T0072371

HOLY PANDEMIC

*Seeking God's Will Amid Sickness,
Death and, Dissension*

MARVIN R. WAMBLE

WESTBOW
PRESS®
A DIVISION OF THOMAS NELSON
& ZONDERVAN

WestBow Press books may be ordered through booksellers or by contacting:

WestBow Press
A Division of Thomas Nelson & Zondervan
1663 Liberty Drive
Bloomington, IN 47403
www.westbowpress.com
844-714-3454

ISBN: 979-8-3850-0848-3 (sc)
ISBN: 979-8-3850-0850-6 (hc)
ISBN: 979-8-3850-0849-0 (e)

Library of Congress Control Number: 2023918156

Print information available on the last page.

WestBow Press rev. date: 11/02/2023

CONTENTS

CHAPTER 1

IT'S KNOCKING ON OUR DOOR

Pastor Quentin Dillard neared the crescendo of his sermon. He stalked the pulpit area like a kingly lion, wiping the sweat rolling down his forehead with the white towel draped across his shoulder. Roaring into his earpiece microphone, Quentin unleashed the message with the highs and lows of gigantic ocean waves. Oh, he was on fire.

He stopped suddenly as he noticed Mother Harriett Marvel slowly making her way down the church's center aisle. She walked with small steps, slightly hunched over like a weight heavier than life was pressing on her shoulders. She appeared to be fighting back tears. Quentin, called Pastor Q by most in his congregation of Greater Faith Temple of Praise, slowly walked down to where Mother Harriett knelt sobbing at the altar. Ushers quickly surrounded her. Some gently laid their hands on her back, while others flapped funeral home fans in her face.

Quentin knelt next to her and turned off his microphone. "What's wrong, Mother Harriett?"

"It's my husband, Frank. He's so sick," she whispered, dabbing her eyes with a white handkerchief.

Mother Harriett was one of the church's older members, having crossed the threshold of eighty several years earlier. She had been involved in many ministries, but her sickness and commitment to caring for her husband of fifty-eight years had taken her out of the church for a while. She had lost a lot of weight. She moved much slower than she once had, but everyone who had been at Greater Faith for any amount of time knew Mother Harriett and her husband.

"He has high blood pressure *and* diabetes," she said, "and he started coughing a week ago and couldn't stop. Then he had trouble breathing. I had to take him to the hospital. You know he didn't want to go." She smiled tearily, shaking her head. "The doctors told him he had the virus. He's been in the hospital for four days, and we don't have any insurance. I'm so scared. I don't know what to do."

Quentin placed his hand on Mother Harriett's frail back as she trembled and cried. It was a sign of compassion parishioners had seen many times from their pastor, who was in his eighth year as the church's spiritual leader. He had taken the pastoral duties after his father, Bishop Cornell Dillard, the founder and overseer of Greater Faith, suffered a serious stroke. Greater Faith was one of the largest Pentecostal churches in the city.

Quentin turned on his microphone and stood up to address the audience. "Sister Harriett's husband, Brother Frank, is in the hospital, and they don't have health insurance. He has contracted COVID-19 and is very sick, but we're going to pray for his healing right now because we know that prayer changes things."

Boisterous amens from the congregation bounced off the ceiling and walls.

The organ flared a chord, and Quentin began to pray. Many of the four hundred in the sanctuary held their hands toward Mother Harriett as the pastor called on the power of the Holy Ghost to touch and heal Brother Marvel and strengthen her. Cries of "yes, Lord" filled the church as the pastor's prayer rose toward the heavens. When he finished, he hugged Mother Harriett, who managed another smile. She began slowly walking to her seat.

"Hold on, Mother Harriett," the pastor said. "We're not finished yet." He gave his head usher a nod. "Mother Harriett, we are the body of Christ. You're going to leave this church today and tell someone God is still in the miracle-working business."

People across the sanctuary yelled "amen" and "that's right."

"So, we are going to take an offering." Like a well-oiled machine, the ushers came to the front of the church, holding large baskets. Quentin reached into his pocket and pulled out a hundred-dollar bill. "I'm going to start this offering with one hundred dollars, and I believe at least ten other people here are blessed and have been moved to bless Mother Harriett with the same. Reach into your purses, empty those pockets, and come on up. And God has a special blessing for you."

Five men and three women made their way to the front of the church, some bringing cash and others writing checks. One of the assistant pastors handed Quentin a bottle of holy oil. Each person who gave was blessed with the laying on of hands.

"Oh, the Holy Ghost is moving right now," Quentin said. "God told us to help those in need. Jesus said, 'What you do for the least of these, you do for me.' I believe ten people here have seventy-five dollars to give. I know you didn't *plan* to give it today. And I know you already gave your tithes, but if you've got it and the Lord is moving in your heart, please come forward. Know that the Lord will bless your sacrifice. Give so the windows of heaven will be opened in your lives."

This was a traditional way of helping the needy at Greater Faith. Quentin had done it many times, and his father had been known to make similar requests. As the offering continued, Quentin called for those who would give fifty, twenty-five, and ten dollars. In about twenty minutes, it seemed that everyone in the church had given to this special offering. After a song and a few announcements, the pastor announced that they had raised $4,200 for Brother Frank's medical expenses. There was loud applause.

"We're too close now," Quentin said. "Mother Harriett is not leaving here with less than five thousand dollars in her purse." The organist hit another screeching note. Shouts of praise bounced throughout the sanctuary. Quentin reached into his pocket and pulled out another hundred-dollar bill. "We only need seven hundred dollars."

Eric Winston came down the aisle, but he wasn't carrying anything in his hand. He walked up to Quentin and whispered, "Pastor Q, I don't carry cash. Is there any way I can use my debit card?"

Quentin gave him a strange look and whispered, "We ain't no bank. We're a church. You know you have to bring cash or a check to the church."

"But I want to give," Eric said adamantly.

"Then you need to find an ATM and get back to church before this offering is over." Quentin smiled as he dismissed Brother Eric. "Come," he said to the congregation.

One of the deacons stood up, holding bills, and walked toward the front of the church. "We only need six hundred dollars, Pastor."

Within five minutes, they had raised another thousand dollars. Mother Harriett waved her frail hand, praising God as tears rolled down her face. The shouting music began, and several congregation members danced into the aisles, giving God glory. The sounds of clapping hands and tambourines filled the sanctuary.

"That's the God we serve," roared Quentin. He cut a quick holy dance as the music rose to another level, unleashing a holy frenzy that was the norm in this high-spirited Pentecostal church. This was the way they celebrated the moves of God.

Quentin did not finish his sermon, but his break with protocol was not unusual. He loved his people and tried to follow God's will in each week's service. That sometimes meant short, Spirit-filled services. On other days, he might preach for more than an hour. He unashamedly followed the unction of the Holy Ghost. After the celebration, which lasted about fifteen minutes, Quentin closed the service. He knew that what God had intended for that day had taken place. The people left happy, stepping into the chill of the late-February day, rejoicing and praising God.

Quentin greeted many members of the congregation as they exited the church. He had a short meeting with first-time visitors, which was always a highlight of his Sunday afternoons. As he went to his office to shower and rest, he saw his friend and church treasurer, Marcel Jacobs.

"That's why we have church," Quentin said with a big smile as he high-fived his friend. "We're here to share the love of Jesus. That is what the people need to see. That's our faith and God's love in action."

After resting in his office for a few minutes following the service, he heard a knock on the door. Before Quentin could move to open it, his father, Bishop Dillard, strolled in, leaning on his cane, which he'd depended on since his stroke. Bishop Dillard had not been the pastor at Greater Faith for many years, but he still wielded tremendous influence in the church he had nurtured since its inception.

"What's up, Pops?" Quentin asked, greeting his father with his favorite term of endearment.

"Doing good today, son. That was a powerful service. It was great you could help Harriett and Frank, longtime members, and good people."

"That was all God," Quentin insisted.

"But tell me, did you give them the entire offering?"

"Of course, I did," Quentin replied. "What was I supposed to do?" Bishop Dillard sat in a chair on the opposite side of Quentin's desk. He turned to make sure the door was closed. "Look, anytime you raise an offering like that, you should hold back at least ten percent. It's sort of the tithe that goes to the church."

"But the money was raised for Mother Harriett and Brother Frank," Quentin insisted.

"She still would have walked outta here with five thousand, which is more than she came in here with," his father said. "But you gotta take care of you. That would have been a quick and easy five hundred dollars in your pocket."

Quentin paused for a second and asked, "Is that what you used to do?"

Bishop Dillard eased back in the chair. "Look, like you, I was never on salary. I had to find creative ways to take care of the family. I don't think God considered it robbery if I took a percentage of those special offerings. I was His servant."

"But that's not why the people were giving. The offering was specifically to help her situation. Anything else is stealing," Quentin said.

Bishop Dillard rolled his eyes and stood up slowly. "You're the pastor. Do what you want to do. I was trying to teach you how we survive in this business."

Quentin frowned. "I don't look at this as a business. To me, it's a calling. And I don't have to take money intended for someone else. I believe by faith that God will take care of me, my family, and my church."

Bishop Dillard turned his back and walked toward the door. "Whatever. You'll learn."

In early March, Quentin considered putting his cell phone in a shredder. He had grown weary of answering calls that delivered nothing but bad news. Earlier in the day, he was told that three high-ranking members of his church's denomination, the Charismatics for Christ (CFC), had been hospitalized with COVID-19 symptoms, including Mother Bertha Shears, who was considered the matriarch of the denomination. He could not believe what was happening. As he sat in his home office, Quentin refilled his glass of red wine and stared at his cell phone as it vibrated. It was a call from one of the members of his church.

"Hello, this is Pastor Q."

"Pastor, this is Sister Justine." The woman's voice was weak and shaky. "I was calling to tell you that Daddy's in the hospital. He's not doing well. He can't breathe or smell nothing. He shoulda gone to the hospital days ago, but you know how stubborn Black men are when it comes to going to the hospital. And we just had to drop him off; none of us could go in. We don't know what's happening. This is the craziest thing I have ever seen." She began to weep. "How can God allow this to happen?"

Quentin had become far too accustomed to these calls. With more than a thousand members in his congregation and close to a million members of their denomination worldwide, he was getting daily news of infections, hospitalizations, and deaths. His stomach bubbled as he searched for an answer he had not found in the past month as the COVID-19 pandemic escalated. Now it was getting close, knocking on the very doors of his church that he had refused to close. Like most in the CFC, Greater Faith had decided to continue having live worship services despite warnings and the closing of most churches in the city.

"Sister Justine, I can't answer that right now," Quentin said. "All I can do is continue to pray for your father, you, your family, and all the families of the church. Know that you are not alone. Unfortunately, they don't even let pastors in the hospitals. But know that God is there. He will care for your father. Our God is a healer, and God is in control. Do you believe that?"

"I don't know anymore, Pastor," she replied in a low voice wrapped with doubt. "I don't know what God is doing. Too many people are getting sick and dying. Good people. God's servants. Did you hear Mother Shears is gone?"

"Yes, I heard."

"Something ain't right, Pastor. Something ain't right."

"All I can tell you is that God will make a way," Quentin said confidently. "You need to get back to your family and let them know that the Greater Faith family is praying for them, and if there is anything they need, we're available. I'll call to check on your father tomorrow. Does he have his cell phone with him in the hospital?"

"Yes."

"Now you be strong in the Lord and the power of His might. Do what your father would want you to do. God's blessings are with you."

"Thank you, Pastor. And make sure you tell the bishop. He and Daddy are good friends."

"I will certainly let Bishop Dillard know. Be blessed now."

Quentin ended the call and exhaled deeply. He turned his phone off, not wanting to receive any more bad news. He heard the door of his office open and looked up to see his wife, Vanessa. He calmly closed the lid of his laptop.

"You all right, baby?" she asked.

"I'm anything but all right," he replied. "People are dying all around us. We're supposed to be God's chosen people, but everyone is dying. Bishops and deacons and pastors, my God. Sister Justine just called and told me her father is in the hospital. I got three of those calls today. These are older people with preexisting conditions. Most over seventy don't make it. Maybe I should have—"

"Now, Quentin, you can't start blaming yourself," Vanessa said in a calm, soothing tone. "There is no way you could have known this would happen."

"But I'm the shepherd God chose to lead these people. And a shepherd is supposed to protect the sheep. Did I miss something? Did I miss a word?" Quentin dropped his head and sighed.

Vanessa had never seen Quentin like this in the nine years they had been married. He was always the strong one. She remembered when their second child, Kyra, was born prematurely. While others around him were falling apart, he stayed calm, praying constantly and declaring her healing. And when his father had the stroke, the church was in a frenzy. Quentin reluctantly took the reins of the church and led with boldness and courage despite the opposition from many of the older members. But Vanessa could see the effects of this virus were wearing him down.

"Baby, you know that God is going to work this out," said Vanessa, who served as a calming influence for Quentin in times of high stress and trouble. It was no accident that her degree was in clinical psychology. She was worried too, but she focused on getting Quentin's head straight so he could seek the Lord and help the people.

"I know God can, but when?"

She smiled and gave him a look that was an answer without words, another one of Vanessa's gifts.

"I know, I know," he said. "I'll understand it better by and by."

So many scenarios were dancing in Quentin's head, making it hard for him to concentrate and difficult to get to sleep. He spent hours staring at his laptop, trying to find peace.

Despite the requests from state and local government officials to close the church, Quentin continued to lead worship services. He asked congregation members to wear masks and warned them of the dangers of singing without facial coverings, but most masks were pulled down during service as congregants continued praising God in traditional ways. They were told to social distance, but all that melted away when the music started. It was like they had not a care in the world.

By mid-April, church attendance was down, primarily because COVID-19 fear was lurking everywhere. Deaths and infections from the virus headlined the news every day, and numbers were climbing. Church members were trying to figure out how to quarantine at home. Many members stopped giving, and Quentin knew the longer the virus spread, the worse things would be at Greater Faith.

Quentin's reasons for continuing to have live worship services were not purely theological. He espoused the virtues of Hebrews 10:25, which promoted a mandate that the saints assemble. He preached that the duty of those who loved Jesus was to continue gathering and praising together. But every time he reviewed the weekly finance report, he knew the church was approaching deep and dangerous waters. He did not believe he could close the church and survive. Several nearby churches that had closed during the embryonic stages of the virus were on the brink of foreclosure.

Greater Faith had money in reserves, but no one had seen this type of economic crisis. The church moved quickly to establish online giving, but members were holding on to the money they would typically give to the church. With a huge first and second mortgage, plus salaries and monthly utilities, Quentin did not know how long the church could hold on. He believed having live services was his best chance to stay ahead of the bills.

Quentin's situation was in limbo too. Because of a long-standing church tradition that he had fought from the first day he became pastor, he was not paid a salary. He received a small weekly stipend that did little more than put gas in his car. He also benefited from funds raised for him during several special days of giving during the year, including his birthday, the pastor's anniversary, pastor's appreciation month, and Christmas. The mortgage on his home and payments on two cars also influenced his decision to keep the church open, though he believed God would provide no matter what.

"By the way, Reggie Bliss called you three times today," Vanessa said. "He called me to say he couldn't get through on your phone."

Quentin took a sip of his drink.

"Why do you spend so much time in here staring at your laptop?" Vanessa asked. "That's not going to help you hear from God. The people of Greater Faith depend on you. And no matter what others say, I believe God raised you for a time like this."

"Thank you, baby," Quentin said softly, closing his laptop. "But I'm gonna tell you, I don't know what God is doing with me or anybody else."

"That's not what you preach," Vanessa said.

"I preach what I have to preach," he said. "I need to encourage the people. That's my assignment. No matter how I'm feeling, I must be the eternal optimist for them. I am their torch bearer of hope. I've got to be the one screaming that everything's gonna be all right. But sometimes I don't know if *I* believe that. It gets dark sometimes," he said, patting his chest.

"Well, you need to find the light. You're the light for so many people. We can't have you going dim. Just keep praying, and God will answer," Vanessa said.

Quentin had been on an amazing journey in the past few years, one he had never imagined. He had not felt prepared to take over the church when his father got sick. He had just received his degree in marketing and advertising. His career had looked promising after being selected for a special marketing program that provided training and a corporate position with an agency. After watching his father's struggles with the church and the denomination, he wanted no part in leading the church, especially as a pastor. But he discovered God had another plan, which eventually led him to the pulpit at Greater Faith.

He'd had no plans to pastor, no strategy to purchase a new church and relocate to the suburbs, and no blueprint to shape a diverse church with a thousand members. It was like he had jumped on a fast-moving train and had no idea where it was headed.

After a rocky start to his pastoral ministry, the church had tripled in size over six years, and the number of ministries skyrocketed, including community programs that helped the hungry, homeless, and undereducated, which had garnered state-wide attention. Quentin preached two services every Sunday and held Saturday night worship services two times a month. Now he was tired and worried. With each call about another COVID-19 victim, he was more confused. The feud with his father didn't help.

"You movin' too fast, boy. You movin' too fast," his father had often told him before COVID-19. "I know you doing good, and money is rolling in, but this new church puts you millions of dollars in debt. I still don't know how you got the money."

"It's like you always taught me, Pops: the Lord will make a way."

"That's not what I'm hearing," the bishop had said hauntingly. "Word on the street is there's some funny money involved. And you know God don't like that."

"Are you talking to me?" Quentin asked, remembering previous conversations with his father about the church's money. "It's all God's money, Pops. We'll be fine."

Cornell was not only a man of profound wisdom, but he was also well-connected. He had been shocked when Quentin signed the paperwork for the new twelve-acre church campus, complete with a five-hundred-seat sanctuary, ten classrooms, a bookstore, a childcare center, a banquet-style fellowship hall, and a small lake on the property. The worst part for Cornell was that the purchase of the new church had taken the Greater Faith out of the inner city. Despite the large attendance and diverse faces from every race, color, and socioeconomic class, Cornell was upset because Greater Faith was no longer the cozy African American Pentecostal church he had built.

"We are supposed to be a Black church, son. That's what Greater Faith has always been," Cornell had told Quentin.

"So you're saying because we have white, Hispanic, Asian, and African members of the church, we're doing something wrong?"

"There is something special that happens when *Black* people worship together," Cornell had insisted.

"Are you telling me that there will not be diversity in heaven?" Quentin had asked, pushing back against his father's notion of race and religion. "Is our heavenly worship of God going to be divided by race? I believe Greater Faith, as it is currently constructed, is the perfect representation of God's Kingdom, *all* people worshipping together."

"I'm praying for you son, but you're awful arrogant," his father had countered. "And the Bible is clear that pride comes before the fall. I've been teaching you that your whole life. We gotta be humble before the Lord, who will bless us."

Quentin could not remember all the lessons his father had given him throughout his life. He believed it was a Southern thing. His father had grown up dirt poor in Alabama under the stern guidance of his father, Absalom, a circuit preacher who could not read or write. Absalom had grown up during the Depression, though he had been quick to say, "Black folks didn't know anything about that 'cause their life was always depressed." Absalom had felt his duty was to pass down all the wisdom he had compiled through the years. He was a great storyteller, weaving tales of working the cotton fields, picking tobacco, making corn liquor, and trying to keep from getting lynched. Every story had a motto or a nugget of wisdom that was more valuable than gold. Most of his tales had concluded with the awesome works of a God, who could not fail. Cornell had continued his father's tradition of storytelling and lesson-sharing, many times to Quentin's dismay.

"I've been humble," Quentin insisted.

"You just built a new house out there in the burbs. You driving that fancy foreign car. Every suit you wear is custom-made, and all the shoes I've worn in my lifetime cost less than two pairs of those fancy brogans you put on your feet. You gotta slow down. The devil is lurking."

Quentin had often heard the stories of his father's life in the South, which was so different from his life on the upper East Coast. Cornell was so hard on Quentin because he'd grown up in a four-room house that he shared with his four brothers and two sisters. They never had much, and as the youngest boy, he had lived his life in hand-me-downs. He was fortunate to get a decent education and had joined the Army, which helped him escape the South. But those memories of struggling were paramount in shaping how Cornell lived. Ministry was the mask hiding Cornell's hunger for money, power, and stability.

"Pops, you too old-school," Quentin had replied. "This is how *we* do it. This is how God has blessed us. All the glory for all I have done belongs to God, and I don't ever forget that. Just relax and see the wonders of *my* God, the God of the twenty-first century."

As the virus raged, Quentin remembered the humble beginnings of a sickness many had thought was a mild form of pneumonia. When the rumblings about the coronavirus started in late January, it was a disease ravaging China and other places overseas. Quentin and most of his CFC colleagues had not paid it any attention.

He was looking forward to the pastor's appreciation recognition in May and the celebration of his eighth anniversary as pastor. Though he wanted to look at the event as a commemoration of how far the church had come, Quentin had to admit he was looking forward to the multitude of gifts he would receive from the congregation and guests. His yearly anniversary celebration was one of his biggest paydays of the year.

The anniversary gala was spectacular, despite the escalating infection and death rate in the United States because of the COVID-19 virus. More than five hundred people came to the celebration, which spanned four days and included a dinner, a gospel concert, and a two-day revival packed with big names and the top dignitaries in the CFC. It was a grand celebration at Greater Faith that weekend, but people started getting sick a week later. Greater Faith continued to hold live services, where Quentin and other ministries laid hands on those in need, soaked everyone with holy oil, and had a Holy Ghost good time in the Lord. But reports of sickness continued.

Just before the fourth Sunday in May, Quentin got word that the police were planning to come to the church to stop the worship service, which had been classified by the county as a superspreader event. Quentin was ready to close the doors because he knew a confrontation with police and local officials would be all over the news. He was not looking for that kind of publicity. As usual, the news reached his father, who paid his son a visit at the church.

It was always strange when his father came to the office. He walked in like he owned the place. Every staff member paid homage to the bishop, who had done so much for so many through the years.

Quentin was caught off guard when his father walked in. He quickly closed the lid of his laptop. "I'm sorry, sir, but I don't believe you have an appointment to see the pastor. You will have to come back another time," Quentin said in jest.

"If I come back, I'm bringing a belt, a rifle, and your momma," Cornell replied quickly. "Choose your punishment."

They both laughed.

"How did you get out here?" Quentin asked.

"You know Darnell is my chauffeur. He's in the sanctuary, probably sleeping." Darnell was Quentin's cousin and often drove his father around town.

Before sitting, the bishop looked approvingly at the many pictures on the wall that traced the church's history. He leaned on his cane, nodded, and smiled as he experienced a "look where He brought me from" moment.

"What's on your mind, Pops? I know you just weren't in the neighborhood 'cause you hate coming out here to the 'burbs."

"No. My trip was intentional because I know you're probably considering closing the church."

"I gotta think about it," Quentin replied. "Every church around here has already gone to exclusively online services. And this virus is wreaking havoc. And, in reality, I'm not closing the church; I'm closing the *building*. There's a difference."

"Son, let me tell you about the time the Ku Klux Klan let it be known they were gonna come to our church with bad intentions," his father said as he eased into a chair.

He'd once been a strong and robust man, but age and illness had reduced his size, though not his voice or his heart. His hair was white, but he still sported a semi-Afro, which signaled his independence. He had lost more than fifty pounds in the last few years, but his spurts of energy brought back memories of who he once was.

"I could've closed the church down. We could've tucked our tails and run, but I knew God was on our side."

"You had church that Sunday?"

"Doggone right we did," Cornell said with a "I remember the day" smile. "Now I'll admit that every usher and all my deacons were packin' that Sunday morning." He laughed. "I was packin' too. And we had lookouts all over the community, but we weren't gonna let nobody keep us from praising God."

"You think I should keep having church even with all these folks getting sick?"

"You've got to," his father responded matter-of-factly. "You have no other choice. This is what God has called you to do. No matter what, God is always going to protect His children We assemble to let others know that we serve the awesome God, who is greater than any pandemic. Look, God has built this church, and the gates of hell will not prevail against it. That's word right there."

"But what about all the people getting sick in churches all around the country?" Quentin asked. "I got five people in the hospital with the virus and countless others who are sick and won't go to the hospital, especially the men."

"They are only sick to prove that God is a healer," Cornell responded. "Just pray. They're gonna be all right."

Quentin was torn. The theology from the church said that God would protect them from all plagues or diseases, but his spirit was speaking another language. Maybe this was different. Plus, he needed people in the seats because the bills kept coming. Big bills.

CHAPTER 2

WHAT A MESS

By early June, the church was in an uproar. Several members demanded to have a full church meeting to discuss how the church was to move forward as the pandemic continued to escalate. That was not how things were done at Greater Faith. When problems arose, the pastor would have a discussion with the church board, a hand-picked group of four men and three women who were loyal to him. The board had several volatile discussions about the future of the church, but as always, Quentin made the final decision, even if he chose to go against his board.

During one of the board meetings, Berniece Jones burst into the room. She was visibly upset. Everyone at the table knew Berniece. She was a lifelong member of the church, a leader of the education ministry, and one whose tongue was as sharp as a two-edged Ginsu knife.

"I need to talk to the pastor, and no, I am not waiting," she snapped.

"Now, Sister Berniece," Deacon Malachi Johnson said, standing slowly. "You know this is not the way things are done. If you have a complaint or an issue, please send it to the board in writing, and we'll discuss it and get back to you."

"Sit yo' tail down, Malachi. I didn't come in here to talk to you.

I came in here to talk to the pastor," she said, lacing each word with a confrontational attitude that caused Deacon Johnson to take his seat. "They just told me that my mother has the virus," she said with a slight crack in her voice. "And I know she got it here 'cause she only left the house to come to church. And you know you shouldn't be open."

"Sister Berniece, how do you know she got it here?" Sister Angela asked. "This virus is everywhere."

Berniece's gaze could have started a fire. "She wasn't sick. All she had was a little sugar and high blood pressure, but she was doing fine," she said. "My mother never left the house, but she *had to come to church*. She had to worship God like she always did. Now she's clinging to life 'cause y'all was huggin' and singing and shouting, and most of the people in here wasn't wearing no mask. And people were in the sanctuary coughing and sneezing. You was acting like nothing was happening in the world. And this is where she got it. And I'm holding you responsible. If she dies, I'm suing the church and every one of you."

Quentin signaled that the board should leave the room so he could talk to Berniece privately. They reluctantly exited under Berniece's piercing stare. "Please sit down, Sister Berniece. I am so sorry to hear about Mother Jeffcoat. You know that we are praying for her healing. And God is a powerful healer."

Berniece sat at the table a few chairs away from the pastor and rolled her eyes. She had known Quentin all his life. She'd been one of his Sunday school teachers, though they had never gotten along.

"Just stop, li'l Quentin," she said bluntly. "I've known you too long for you to try to butter me with your smooth words. I ain't no yeast biscuit. My mother is in the hospital dying. From what I hear, we have ten or twelve others in the hospital and more sick folks who are quarantined in their homes."

Quentin tried to stay calm, not realizing that the news had spread through the congregation. "There is little doubt that we are under attack," he said stoically, looking Berniece in the eye. "The devil is trying to stop our worship. He knows that we gain power when two or three are gathered. But we're not going to let that happen. It is our obligation to assemble as saints of God and give God praise."

Berniece leaned forward in her chair and glared at the pastor. "You're killing people. Do ya hear me? You're killing people. If you keep this up, they gonna come arrest you for first degree murder 'cause every planned service is premeditated," she snapped. "Your father would never have allowed this to happen. I wish you were half the man your father is"

That stung, but Quentin knew many older church members felt that way. The bishop still had tremendous influence, not only at Greater Faith but also in the other churches in the denomination that had remained open. When he had his stroke, he'd left big shoes to fill.

"What do you want me to do, Sister Berniece?" Quentin asked. "I would love to visit your mother and pray with her, but they aren't allowing us in the hospitals. She is in our prayers, but how can I bring *you* peace?"

"You just better hope that Momma don't die because you will not have *any* peace. But for God's sake, stop having church. You're inviting people to their own funerals. It was my mother this time, but yo' momma comes to church too. And the bishop, as sick as he's been, sho'nuff needs to stay away from here."

"Now, Sister Berniece—"

"Talk to my hand li'l Quentin Dillard, Pastor," she said, holding up her hand and turning her head. "If you ain't gonna tell me you're closing the church, I don't wanna hear nothing you've got to say. This should be an easy choice: close the church. I don't know why you won't, but you need to do something, or the hospital gonna have more of your members than the church does on Sunday morning."

She stood up and stared at him. "Since you was a boy, you've always been slow," she said, shaking her head in disgust. "I prayed the Lord would pour some accelerant in your spirit, but your mind is still sputtering like someone put water in your gas tank."

She turned and walked slowly out of the boardroom.

Quentin informed the board that the meeting was over. Only his treasurer and longtime friend, Marcel Jacobs, remained. Marcel and Quentin had been friends since middle school. They played Little League baseball together, played in the high school band, and hung out in church for years. Of all the board members, Quentin relied on Marcel to steer him in the right direction.

"Hey, man, I think we need to close the church," Quentin said as Marcel took a deep breath and sat down at the long table.

"You can't," Marcel said.

"Sister B is right; we're killing people," Quentin admitted, obviously touched by his discussion with Berniece.

"Q, you need to understand. If we don't keep bringing in the money, there are people who are going to kill you *and* me."

Quentin closed his eyes. "Can't we just talk to them? How can they expect us to come up with all that money during a global pandemic?"

"It would be different if we were dealing with a bank or a traditional loaning institution," Marcel said. "But we're dealing with a vicious individual. If you're expecting him to show compassion, you foolin' yourself."

"I'll have to pray about it," Quentin said.

"You can pray all you want," Marcel said. "But you got two weeks to come up with the payment. And the daily interest on late payments is mind-boggling."

"I knew I shouldn't have cut that deal," Quentin lamented.

"It was great at the time," Marcel admitted. "We were rolling in dough. Attendance was up. Giving was up. We had the money set aside for two or three payments. But this COVID thing is like Roundup: it's killing everything. At least that's what they're saying. I still don't think it's real."

Quentin looked at his friend. "Oh, it's real. You need to watch the news instead of all those housewives shows. People are dying all over the world. And we have at least fifteen people and counting in the hospital and over a dozen in quarantine all because we keep having live church services."

"Think about it," Marcel said. "People get sick all the time. Of all the people they say have this virus, some of them may have the flu or something they were going to get anyway. And as for the deaths, people been dying every day since I can remember."

Quentin could not believe what he was hearing, but knowing his friend, his thoughts about the virus were not completely out of the range of his possibilities. Quentin's phone began to vibrate. He did not want to answer, but he saw it was his mother.

"Hey, man, let me take this. It's Mom."

Marcel stood up to leave the room. "Tell Mother Dillard I said hello."

Quentin knew something was serious. Though he and his mother talked several times a week, she rarely called him. She felt it was her child's responsibility to check on Momma.

"Hey, Momma. How you doing today?"

"I'm doing good for an old lady. Are you at the church?"

"Yeah, I just had a board meeting."

"Well, come by here on the way home. We need to talk."

"Can't you talk to me now?"

"No. I need to see your face."

"Why don't you FaceTime me?" he said, laughing softly.

"You know good and well I don't do none of that FaceTime mess. I need to see you up close and personal. Dinner is at six." She hung up.

"But I have a few more meetings—" He realized she was no longer on the phone. He knew he wasn't going to win that argument anyway.

Quentin always drifted into flights of nostalgia when he visited his childhood home, which his parents had lived in for more than forty years. He had lived in the small three-bedroom house with his parents for the first eighteen years of his life. Even at the height of Greater Faith under Bishop Dillard's pastorate, the couple, who had been married for forty-seven years, had never considered moving from their first home. His father was urged to buy a larger house to demonstrate to the congregation the vastness of God's blessings for the flock's leader, but the bishop had been steadfast: "This is the home that God gave me and Essie, and I will not be moved." Quentin did not know if his father loved the house or was trying to be obedient to God, or was just too cheap to buy a more expensive home.

Quentin had not lived there for more than twenty-five years, but his old key still worked. His nose was tickled by the smell of fried chicken and greens the minute he opened the door. He walked through the living and dining rooms, which were always dark and cold unless the family had company. The action in this house always occurred in the rear of the home, where his parents spent most of their time in the kitchen and den.

The living room was always impeccable, with a white eighteenth-century style sofa and love seat with clear plastic covers. Old *Ebony* and *Black Enterprise* magazines still covered the small coffee table in the middle of the room. The dining room housed an eight-foot table with a large cherry China cabinet and hutch.

Quentin had spent lots of agonizing hours at that table. During his adolescent years, it was his desk. It was where he discovered his love for reading and his disdain for math, algebra, and calculus. Quentin had always been more nerd than athlete, though he enjoyed watching sports with his father. His true love was reading. The books he was given in school only mildly entertained him; he had gotten the most enjoyment from reading his father's books by Howard Thurman and James Baldwin. Obsessive reading had helped Quentin attain academic honors in high school and awards during his collegiate studies. He had never planned to be a pastor, but he was always interested in the church's potential to help people in poor communities. Many social justice ideologies espoused by theologians like Thurman had slipped to the back burner when he became a pastor, but he knew that in the end he wanted the church to help struggling people while promoting a relationship with Jesus.

When he pushed open the swinging door to the kitchen, the temperature rose at least ten degrees, and the bright lights seemed to darken Quentin's transition lenses. The smells of heavenly food blanketed his face like a mask. He knew his father would be sitting in his easy chair, watching sports on TV. In many cases, however, the TV would be watching his dad, who took pride in taking frequent naps.

Despite her seventy-six years, when his mother was cooking, she moved like an African dancer with a smile on her face and determination in her eyes. Quentin rushed in to greet his mother with his usual hug and kiss, but she held up a frying pan and backed away.

"Boy, I don't know where you been. You might be bringing the rona up in here. Now go sit down at the table and use some hand sanitizer. And you oughta be wearing a mask. It's good to see you, and I love you, but we ain't doin' no huggin' today."

Quentin was taken aback. "Come on, Momma. I'm your son. I'm rona free. I can at least get a hug."

She waved the frying pan. "You can come near me if you want to, but you gonna be huggin' that floor."

He shook his head and sat down at the table as directed. To his surprise, his father was not in the den. "Where's Pops?"

"He's resting in the bedroom. He hasn't had a lot of energy lately. I think all this sickness and death of his friends is getting to him." His mother looked at him and frowned. "Are you gettin' fat?"

"Momma, every time I see you, you tell me that either I'm getting, or I got fat, but I haven't gained a pound in six months."

"Well, maybe you need to get some bigger clothes. Men your size shouldn't be wearing no skimpy jeans."

Quentin did not consider himself a big man. He stood five feet ten and would be forever upset that he didn't reach six feet. He had gained weight over the years, but he thought he held his two hundred pounds well.

"These are not *skinny* jeans, and my clothes fit fine. Maybe you should have that cataract surgery you've been putting off for years."

"I can see just fine," she snapped. "You hungry?"

Quentin knew that even if he was not hungry, he was going to have to eat. His mother, a Louisiana native, took pride in her cooking. She was known for her incredible meals and willingness to feed hundreds of people. This was one of the few times he would have a one-on-one meal with her. She put his two favorite pieces of fried chicken on his plate with greens and her nobody-does-it-better potato salad. He knew he was in for a treat. He picked up the breast and prepared to bite into a little piece of heaven.

"I know you ain't thinking about eating in *this* house without saying your grace," his mother snapped, standing over him with her hands firmly planted on her hips. "You left here and turned into a heathen."

He smiled. "I just wanted to see if you were watching."

"Say grace and stop lyin'."

Quentin placed his hands together, lowered his head, and closed his eyes. "God is great, and God is good. Let us thank Him for our food. Amen."

He opened one eye to look at his mom.

"Boy, just eat. How you gonna come in here with the grace we taught you forty years ago. You oughta be shame. And you a big-time pastor. Help him, Lord."

As usual, his mother didn't eat much. She just sat down at the table and watched her son scarf down all the food on his plate. He seemed to eat the entire chicken breast in one bite.

"You better slow down. You eatin' like the police is chasin' you," she said.

Quentin laughed. "I just wanna get mine before Pops comes in."

His mother wiped her hands on her blue apron and adjusted her favorite wig. "So how are things going at the church?" she asked.

"These are strange times, Momma. With this virus getting worse and people at the church getting sick, I don't know if I'm coming or going."

She poured him a glass of sweet iced tea. He smiled as he recognized the tall glass with pictures of ships, his favorite from childhood.

"So why haven't you closed the church?" she asked. "Most of the churches in the city aren't having live services. They're on Doom or something. I tell you, I just couldn't watch no church service on anything called Doom."

"It's called *Zoom*, Momma. And I've been thinking about closing the church, but so many people want to keep it open. Pops said I should never close the church. And we have to believe God will protect us."

She adjusted her wig again, one of her nervous habits. "Have you been reading the newspaper or watching the news on that electronic thing you got? People in churches have been getting sick and dying. Even in our church, long-time saints are dropping like flies in a Raid factory. We got three bishops in the hospital, and I'm hopin' your father ain't got the rona."

"Yeah, I've read the stories, but maybe they don't know God like we do."

"Did you hear what I said, or is all that chicken chompin' blockin' your ears? *Bishops* are sick and in the hospital. Those are the bishops who pray to the same God we do. The bishops who know that God is the ultimate healer. There is something different going on here."

"Maybe God isn't pleased with our bishops or the CFC."

"I don't know about that, but I believe God is speaking to us, but we too caught up to pay attention," she said. "We been so locked into the tradition of always going into the church building, always laying on hands, always believing the Holy Ghost gonna save us, that we might have missed the shift from God. Maybe this *is* God's new thing."

"Naw, Momma, we just gotta keep prayin'."

"When was the last time you read your Bible?" she asked. "This is not the first plague that has come on the people of this earth, and those plagues took out God's people too. Disobedience got us into this mess, and I believe part of what we're supposed to do as children of God is to listen to what the experts say and govern ourselves accordingly. That means you need to close the church and keep your people safe."

Quentin sipped his tea as he considered his response. He agreed with his mother, but extenuating circumstances weighed his decision. "I'm thinking about it, Momma. That's what the board meeting was about today. But they're afraid we'll lose the people if we close the church."

"I been around this church for a long time," she said. "You know good and well this ain't only about the people; it's about the people's money. Tell the truth and shame the devil. But you ain't gonna get no money if everyone in your church is dead."

"You ain't gotta go at it that hard, Momma."

"Boy, when have I ever beat around the bush? I called you here to tell you to close the church. I don't care what the board says, and I don't care what your daddy says or them highfalutin bishops. This thing here is serious. And if you keep them doors open, you gonna have blood on your hands."

Quentin frowned, but his mother was always brutally honest and almost always right. "All right, Momma. I'll start making plans to close the church."

"Ain't no one gonna close the doors of Greater Faith," his father said as he walked slowly into the room. "We cannot neglect the gathering of the saints." He moved toward his Lazy Boy recliner, leaning on his cane. "Good to see you, Q. Now this is a man's decision. Don't be influenced by your mother."

She picked up a chicken drumstick and acted like she was going to throw it at her husband, whose back was to her.

"And don't throw no chicken at me, woman," he said as he flopped into his chair.

"It's a man's decision?" she asked forcefully. "Well, just don't you forget that there would not be one man walking this earth without a woman. And your church would be pretty messed up too, 'cause women run just about everything."

"You can't close the church," his father said as he reached for the TV remote.

"Pops, all the churches are closing. People are getting sick. I know you heard about Mother Sheards," Quentin said. "This might be the time we follow the rules of the land but continue to pray for God's covering and healing."

"You're seriously considering closing the church?" his father asked. "That's monumental. It's never been done."

"Pops, you taught me that as the shepherd of the flock, it is my primary responsibility to keep the people safe. We've got people in the hospital I can't visit. And most of the folks who got sick only came to church. The close contact and singing without masks are killing people."

"You do what you want," his father said in disgust. "But you'll regret it. Once you close, getting it open again will be very difficult. And most of your people won't come back."

"They won't come back if they're dead either," his mother said.

"Do what *you* want," his father said. "It's your church."

The telephone rang, and his mother picked it up. "Bishop Jenkins, it is always a pleasure to hear your voice, but you don't sound too well. Yes, everyone is fine. Nelly's sitting right here. I'll put him on the line." She had called her husband Nelly for as long as Quentin could remember.

"Nelly, it's Bishop Jenkins for you. But he sounds terrible," she said, covering up the mouthpiece." He's wheezing and hacking. I felt sick just talking to him."

Cornell struggled to stand up. Then he picked up the portable phone and walked into his office at the rear of the house.

"Was that *our* Bishop Jenkins?" Quentin asked.

Bishop Jeremiah Jenkins was the presiding bishop of Quentin's church and several others in the area. He and Cornell were old friends.

"Yes, that was our bishop. I'm sure he's just checking on your father. With so much sickness in the church, he probably stays on the phone," his mother said. "He needs some cod liver oil 'cause he sounds bad."

CHAPTER 3

SAY WHAT?

O ver the next few days, Quentin wanted to throw his phone into the nearest river. He always prided himself in being available to his congregants. That had become more and more difficult as the church had grown, but in the past few days, his phone had been on continuous vibration mode. He felt like he was living on an earthquake fault line. He had to pick which calls to answer and which to allow to go to voicemail. This evening was worse than normal.

Finally, he answered the call of an unidentified number who had called five times.

"It's about time you picked up, Pastor Q. I've been calling all day. This is Brother Tony."

Tony Birch was the musician for the Gospel Jubilee Choir, one of five choirs in the church.

"Did you change your number?" Quentin asked, wondering why Tony's name had not appeared on the caller ID.

"When too many people get my number, I just get a new one," Tony said.

"Well, when you get a new number and don't let me know, your name doesn't show on my caller ID," Quentin responded. "And I can't answer every call."

There was a pause. "I never thought about that, but be that as it may, I got some news."

"What news do you have?"

"We've got six members of the choir who are in the hospital with the virus and at least ten who are quarantined at home. I think it might be the result of an … unscheduled rehearsal we had about a week ago."

Quentin closed his eyes and took a deep breath. "That's more than a third of the choir, Brother Tony. Didn't I tell you to suspend all rehearsals?"

"Come on, Pastor Q. You can't just stop God's children from singing. But I did what you told me. I canceled practice and went to church to play the piano; it brings me so much peace. Word got out that I was there, and the next thing I knew, the choir stand was almost full. We just started singing and praising and had a good time. We had to do it. You can't hold back God's praise."

"And now more than half the choir is sick or in the hospital," Quentin said. "You had to?"

"Don't get mad at me. It was not a called rehearsal. It was … a movement of God. Plus, Sister Cee said it was OK."

After hearing the reference to Carretha Henderson, who everyone called Sister Cee, Quentin understood why trouble had raised its ugly head. Carretha was one of the women in the church who claimed to have a prophetic voice. She was always speaking in tongues, laying hands on people, and giving a word from God. Quentin and the CFC believed some people were gifted to be prophets; after all, that was biblical. They just weren't sure that Carretha was one of the gifted.

"What did Sister Cee say this time?" Quentin asked.

There was a long pause. "Well, she told us that God would bless us because we had come to worship Him in this special time in history."

"Is that all?"

Another pause. "And she said that because we were God's chosen, we could take off our masks and sing without fear because we were anointed for this moment."

Quentin took another deep breath. In the back of his mind, he wondered if the church could sue Carretha for slander or malice or something. Several times members of the church had to shut her down because the message she said came from God had been absolute nonsense, but she kept coming back.

"And y'all believed that?"

"Come on, Pastor Q. Everyone knows Sister Cee's got the gift."

"Who said she has the gift? She talks a lot, but I don't know if any of her utterances have come true."

"Now, Pastor, you remember when she said Sister Joan was gonna have a baby boy."

"Brother Tony, she had a fifty percent chance on that one, and Sister Joan had already had three girls."

There was a long silence.

"Where's Sister Cee?" Quentin asked.

"Um, she's at St. Anthony's Hospital. She tested positive and is having a real tough time breathing, I hear."

Quentin could not let that irony pass. "So *she* is in the hospital?"

"Yeah, but she is telling everyone who calls her that this is only a test from God. She has foreseen her healing and the healing of everyone in the choir. She is a strong woman of God, Pastor."

"Here's the deal, Brother Tony. Moving forward, you can't go to the church to practice, pray, or whatever. You are forbidden from getting anyone from our choirs to meet with you or sing with you. Do you understand?"

"Pastor Q, that's kinda hard. You know I don't have a piano, and to keep my skills sharp—"

"Brother Tony!" Quentin yelled. "If you go near the church, I am going to sharpen your skills with a knife. Do you understand?"

"All right, sir. But I don't think that's right."

"You got three words right: 'I don't think.' Let me get off the phone with you so I can check on Sister Cee. And don't let me hear that you came within five miles of the church."

Tony could play the organ, piano, and about five other instruments, but he had never been the smartest instrument in the orchestra. When Quentin first met him, he had thought something was wrong because he was acting very strangely. But he could play, sing, and direct. He was a gold mine of musical talent. Now Quentin was thinking it was fool's gold.

"Brother Tony, send me the list of sick choir members and where they are. I'll call them tomorrow."

"That's a lot of work, Pastor Q."

"What did you say?" Quentin asked with attitudinal punctuation.

"I said I'll get to work on the list immediately."

When Quentin finally found Carretha at the hospital, her voice sounded like it had walked over miles of sandpaper. She was coughing after almost every word, but she stayed true to herself.

"How are you doing, Sister Carretha?"

"Pastor Q," she said, struggling to push out each word. "I am blessed and highly favored of the Lord." She coughed loudly. "I'm blessed by the best and expecting a miracle." She began coughing again.

Quentin just shook his head. "You don't sound too good, Sister Cee. I surely hope you are doing what the doctors tell you."

"Jesus is my doctor," she whispered. "All this medicine and stuff is for nonbelievers. By faith I am healed." She began coughing again.

"Sister Cee, here is what I want you to know, and I want you to listen to your pastor. Jesus *is* a healer, but the Bible doesn't tell us *how* he will heal us. And because we know that God can use anyone, I believe God is using your doctors and nurses to heal you. In fact, I believe these doctors and nurses were placed in the hospital during this season so that you could catch this revelation."

She was quiet.

"But, Pastor—" she whispered.

"No, Sister Cee. You need to allow God to work through the people assigned to you. If you don't follow their directions and help them guide you into this healing, you will be blocking *their* blessings. And I know you don't want to do that."

"No, I don't want to block their blessing," she said, coughing continuously.

"Then be obedient. Take *all* your medicine. Drink your water, rest, and listen for the word of God in this."

She coughed again. "Yes, Pastor. I'll do that."

"Before I go, let's pray." Quentin lifted a passionate prayer. "Now, Sister Cee, God loves obedience. So do what you are supposed to do to ensure you get well. I know that you are going to do that. And we look forward to talking to you when you leave the hospital."

"And how are you doing, Pastor?" she asked, her voice finding strength.

"I'm doing just fine."

"I'm not talkin' about your health; I'm talking about *your* problem."

Quentin was confused. "What are you talking about? Are your meds kickin' in?"

"Come on, Pastor Q. Don't pretend you don't know. And I want you to know that *I* know."

"What are you talking about, Sister Cee?"

"I'm talking about your problem," she said bluntly. "The Bible says what is done in darkness will come to light. And I know you don't want this to come out."

Quentin was silent for a moment. "Are you a hacker or something?"

"No. I am a prayer warrior and a prophetess."

Quentin felt like a baseball bat hit him in the stomach. No one knew, or so he had thought. He had been wrestling with this sin for years. But it had gotten worse during the pandemic and with all the bad news.

"How do you know?"

"You one of those who didn't think I had the gift. But God speaks to me," Carretha said. "God told me about your problem, and I am supposed to tell you it is time to get some help, some professional help, or things could end badly."

"I pray about it all the time. I believe God is going to set me free."

"How's that been going for you?" she asked and then coughed loudly. "Just like you told me I must obey my doctors, you need to see a professional and get some help. If not, you might not make it."

"I'll think about it."

"You need to do more than think about it," she said before coughing again. "You've got to go. The future of your family and the church depend on it. You can't lead God's people chained to the devil's garment."

"You're going to keep this between you and me, aren't you?"

"I won't tell a soul unless you don't get help. I'm your advocate. We all have easily entangled sins that we need to wrestle with, but there are great plans for you, and you cannot allow this sickness to derail God's plan."

"Sister Cee, you have more than I thought you did. And I will get help. I gotta do something."

As he hung up the phone, his mind raced like it was at the Indy 500. He knew he needed help, but he could not stop thinking about the other members of the choir and congregation who were sick and in the hospital. He checked his emails and saw that Tony had sent him the contact information for all the sick choir members. Quentin adjusted his schedule and began calling each one. As he had done so many times, he put his challenge on the back burner. Most of the sick choir members seemed surprised that the pastor would call. He had great conversations and prayers with each member until he called Cedric Boyd, who was in the hospital.

"Pastor Q, they let me in here, but I gotta leave," Cedric said.

"Brother Boyd, what's the hurry?"

"Sooner or later, they gonna ask for my insurance, and I ain't got none. Then they're gonna ask for some cash, and I ain't got none of that either. Now unless this here fancy room is free, I need to get out of here soon."

"Aren't you a veteran?" Quentin asked.

"Yes, I am. Served two tours in Vietnam. Now, I had a little problem with that second tour. I kinda slipped away and didn't tell nobody."

"You went AWOL?" Quentin asked.

"I sure did. Yes, sir. I had to get outta there."

"What happened?"

"Too much madness, too much politics, and too much killing. And I didn't have no gripe with those people. So I slipped away. They finally found me after a couple of weeks and sent me back to the States. I was supposed to go on trial or something like that, but I slipped away again."

"It sounds like you're some kinda criminal."

"I never had any criminal intent, but it don't look so good on paper. That's why I gotta get outta here. When they find out my real name ..."

"Wait a minute," Quentin said. "Cedric Boyd is not your real name?"

"Well, it is and it ain't."

"Say what?"

"It *is* my name 'cause I been using it for the past twenty-four years or so. But it *ain't* the name my momma gave me."

Quentin was shocked. Cedric Boyd, or whoever he was, had come to the church about six years ago. There was little doubt he had gone through bad times. When he first arrived, he had always worn the same clothes to church two or three times a week. He was clean, well-mannered, and always willing to help, but you could tell something was not quite right. For the past few years, he had worked with one of the vets from the church who was everybody's handyman. Boyd received pay under the table and probably hadn't paid taxes or needed a legitimate ID in years.

"Brother Boyd, if you got the virus, you gotta let them help you."

"I don't think I got nothing. I don't feel bad. I can't smell a doggone thing—oh, excuse my language again—but my fever ain't been over 101."

"So, you've had a fever at 100."

"Who ain't had that?" he asked. "You get a little mad, you bustin' over 100. Plus, some of the stuff they gave me in Army messed me up. Ain't no tellin' what I got. But I gotta get outta here. I'd slip out tonight if I could find my clothes."

"It seems like you do a lot of slipping out."

Cedric laughs softly. "Well, when you get in places you shouldn't be, you better learn how to slip out or they'll sho'nuff kill ya. I won't be in here long. You can bet on that."

Quentin prayed with Cedric before preparing to make another call. "Now, Brother Boyd, you stay in touch. You are a part of the Greater Faith family, and we don't want you slippin' away."

Cedric laughed. "No, y'all have treated me well. I ain't going nowhere. My name may change, my face may change, but I love Jesus, and I love Greater Faith."

Later that evening, Vanessa and Quentin had a good time discussing his various conversations during the day. He always shared the ups and downs of his day with his wife. She was a great listener and often had sage advice that he always appreciated. Both were concerned for all those who were sick, and they hoped no one else would fall victim to the virus.

But the calls kept coming. Every day more people were confirmed infected, taken to the hospital, or at home not feeling well. Quentin knew he would have to send a message to his congregation to let them know the status of church members.

As he prepared for bed, he made his usual trip to his computer. He checked to see if Vanessa was sleeping. This was usually his viewing time. As he opened his laptop, Carretha's words echoed in his spirit: *"The future of your family and the church depend on it."* He closed his eyes and prayed a prayer for cleansing and forgiveness. Then he turned off his laptop. It was a prayer he often prayed to no avail. He hoped this time it would stick.

CHAPTER 4

IT'S IN THE BOOK

The weather was hot in the middle of July, and the virus was hotter. Quentin was feeling the heat. It was almost 2:00 a.m. on Sunday morning, and he was still wrestling with the sermon. He normally found peace with what the Lord had given him before midnight, allowing him to have a good night's sleep before the frenzy of Sunday morning services. But this was different. He had to present a strong case, backed by biblical principles, that explained why Greater Faith should be obedient to the demands of the county and state governments, even if that meant closing the church building.

The apostle Paul made the point in Romans 12. Peter said the same thing in 1 Peter 2. The bottom line from both apostles was that we should submit to the government authorities. State and local officials had signed executive orders stating that all houses of worship should be closed. Quentin knew this would be his last sermon in the Greater Faith sanctuary for quite a while.

His attention was drawn away from his laptop when Vanessa came in with a steaming cup of tea. She rarely came to visit during his sermon preparation, but it was good to see her smiling face.

"What are you doing here?" Quentin asked. "I know you didn't bring me coffee at this hour."

She rolled her eyes. "No, this is tea. It's that special mix I told you about to help you sleep."

"You think I need help sleeping?"

"Baby, you haven't had a good night's sleep in weeks. You've been tossing and turning all night. And it's starting to affect you. Your eyes aren't clear, you're losing weight, and it looks like your hair is turning gray."

"My hair is *not* turning gray."

"I'll let you deal with that denial, but you're not sleeping."

"Times are tough, Vee," Quentin said after a deep breath. "People are getting sick and dying in our church, community, and the CFC. And this virus is wreaking havoc everywhere. My God. I've got internal and external pressure to close the church on one hand and demands that I keep the doors open on the other. No matter what I do, people will question my motives and beliefs. What do you think I should do?"

Vanessa sat the tea on his desk and pulled up a chair. She had known Quentin for more than eighteen years, the last thirteen as his wife. They had been through a lot together and were great friends. He knew she would not sugarcoat the situation.

"I know you've been praying," she began. "And in these times, it is often hard to hear from God because there are so many voices and so many distractions. But the Bible is clear. If you follow what is written in God's word, you can't go wrong."

Quentin sipped his tea and leaned back in his chair. "The Bible isn't all that crystal clear either. It tells us not to neglect meeting together. We are also told that where two or three are gathered, that's church."

"That may be church," Vanessa countered, "but it says nothing about a building. Saints can gather anywhere. Two or three do not have to be in a church building to ensure God's presence. And to be truthful, I don't remember Jesus belonging to a church. I know he went to the temple a lot, at least when he was in Jerusalem, but we have mistaken the church for the building."

"Everything you said is true," Quentin sighed. "And I'm ready to close the church building. In fact, today will probably be our last day in the building for who knows how long, but when I think about it, I think I should not be the one closing the church. It should be God."

Vanessa leaned forward to make sure Quentin was looking into her eyes. "Maybe that's what God is doing," she said. "This would not be the first time God made a point with a plague. You always preach that God moves in strange and mysterious ways. You tell us that God's ways are not our ways. So why can't you consider that God *is* closing church buildings during this pandemic so those who say they are His followers can experience something new? Maybe this is a way to reach people who will not come into our church building."

Vanessa had a knack for piercing Quentin with the truth. That had been one of the reasons he was attracted to her when they first met in college. She was deeply spiritual and possessed gifts that allowed her to hear God in a special way. And she was never swayed by Quentin's eloquent articulation, on-time humor, or kingly aura. Vanessa wore many hats. She was a wife and mother, the First Lady of the church, and a fierce protector of her husband. She was not well-liked by many at Greater Faith because of her light complexion, small frame, amber eyes, and bone-straight hair. Still, when she began talking with a strong New York accent that framed her always present "don't mess with me or my family" attitude, there was little doubt that she was much more than a dainty First Lady.

"Maybe God wants us to close these buildings," she said.

"Why?" Quentin asked.

"So, we can be the church again. So, we won't be tripping on the number of people in the pews on Sunday morning or how much the offering was. Maybe God wants us to focus on getting close to Him again and helping people in need."

Quentin lowered the lid of his laptop. "Let's go to bed. This is going to be a big day."

Attendance had been dwindling for Sunday service over the past few weeks. It was obvious that people were worried about close contact with COVID raging. It did not help that the local newspaper had listed Greater Faith, along with several other churches and nightclubs, as a potential superspreader of the virus.

The sanctuary was less than half full when Quentin strolled to the pulpit, carrying a heavy burden. He tried to smile to display his usual joy when he was in service. But his face betrayed him and he revealed an angst most in the congregation had never seen. At this point, the church had been rolling for about thirty minutes with lots of praise, worship, and prayer. Quentin was confident that the word God had given him would touch the people during this unprecedented time in the history of the church, the nation, and the world.

"It is good to see that so many of you decided to come to church this morning," Quentin began. "I welcome all those joining us on Facebook Live, Zoom, YouTube, and the Greater Faith Streaming Network. This is a time when we must exercise extreme caution because the COVID-19 virus is dangerous. As most of you know, most of the churches in the city have closed their doors, and I believe it is time for us to do the same. Today will be the last live service we will have for a while at Greater Faith until the virus is under control."

There was moaning in the audience.

"I don't like it either," Quentin admitted, "but there's too much sickness, and the experts aren't sure how to slow this virus down. As the shepherd of this flock, I am responsible for keeping everyone safe. And I want to ensure that no one else gets infected because they came to Greater Faith."

"But you've been telling us that the Lord will protect us!" someone yelled from the congregation.

Quentin nodded in agreement. "Yes, I have. And God always watches out and protects his children. But I believe God is doing a new thing, certainly something we have never seen before. God is moving us to obey the authorities of the land, which is biblical, so we can have a new and different experience with Him. We always say that we are the church, not the building. I believe we will have an opportunity to see what that *really* means. And despite the number of people from Greater Faith who have been infected, God is protecting us. The situation could be a lot worse."

"So how long are we going be closed?" someone called out.

"I really don't know," Quentin responded. "We will be meeting as much as possible online and over the telephone. We will do all we can to keep you advised of our status. But our church work, ministries, Christian education, and community programs here and at our downtown location will continue to function. We'll just have to figure out how to do them without coming into our buildings. But it can be done, and God is on our side."

As Quentin was talking, he noticed the heads of his congregation looking to his right. When he turned, he was shocked to see Bishop Jenkins walking into the pulpit area with Quentin's father. He lost his train of thought.

"My goodness," Quentin said. "Isn't this a surprise? Our presiding bishop and our overseer have come to join us. Praise the Lord."

Bishop Jenkins, a tall and stout man, placed his fist over his heart and cleared his throat as he walked toward Quentin and took the microphone. "Praise the Lord, everybody," he barked in a deep baritone voice. "Praise the Lord," he said before coughing softly.

Quentin looked at his father, who turned away and joined in the praise. He knew that was not a good sign.

"I have come by this morning to let you know that despite the desire of your pastor, Greater Faith will *not* be closing," Bishop Jenkins said with a smile. There were a few claps before the sanctuary went quiet. People looked confused.

"The board of bishops held an emergency meeting and decided that the churches of the CFC are going to trust in God during this pandemic. We know that God is on our side, and He requires us to assemble weekly and give Him praise. None of our churches will be closing."

Quentin could not believe his ears. He could not remember the bishops' board, the ruling body of the CFC, ever interfering with the workings of the church. In fact, Quentin had very little respect for the Episcopal Board of Bishops, who he thought acted too much like a secret society that looked out for their own interests. He and most of the clergy in the CFC did not trust them, which was difficult for Quentin because his father was a member.

"We will be here next week and every week after that showing the people the power of our God and the Holy Ghost," the bishop said.

Quentin was furious. He signaled his assistant pastor to give him another microphone. The bishop continued to tell the people why the CFC would be a holdout, stating that no weapon formed against them would prosper. Quentin walked to stand next to the bishop.

"No, bishop. I'm sorry," Quentin said forcefully. "I don't care what the bishops' board has ruled. The doors of *this* church will be closed after today. *I* am responsible for these people. And I will not be bullied into keeping these doors open and allowing more people to get sick. Now you can take the church from me if you want, but as long as *I'm* pastor, Greater Faith will be closed for the foreseeable future."

The bishop was shocked. "I am the presiding bishop and—"

"I don't care who you are," Quentin said firmly. "Greater Faith will be closed. We have had more than twenty-five people infected, scores in quarantine, and several are positive they got the virus here. It has got to end."

"Well, I'll just have to bring in a pastor who will be obedient to the board's demands," the bishop said as boos rained down from the congregation.

"You better get a pastor *and* a locksmith," Quentin said, "because this place will be closed."

The bishop called the head deacon to the pulpit. "Can you please escort Rev. Dillard out of the building?" The deacon did not move. "I'm calling on you, Deacon, to remove your pastor by the authority of the board of bishops."

The deacon still did not move.

"Is there anyone here who understands my authority?" the bishop bellowed. "I have every right to remove your pastor." There was chaos in the church. While some in the congregation yelled at the bishop, others walked toward the doors with strides of disgust.

"Bishop, I don't want this to get ugly, so I'll leave," Quentin said. "But I believe you have overstepped the rule of your authority. And I certainly do not believe that God is pleased with what you are doing today. You are disrupting the body of Christ. Why? So you can keep getting paid? We haven't seen you during worship service in three years, and you come here for this? Shame on you."

Quentin walked out of the pulpit. The remaining congregation appeared stunned. Some were crying. Others were shaking their heads.

"We love you, Pastor!" one cried out.

"Don't leave us, Pastor!" screamed another.

The bishop stood there, steaming. "Deacon, you might as well go with him."

The entire ministerial staff of three assistant pastors and four deacons stood and followed the pastor out of the sanctuary, along with several other members of church leadership.

"I am sorry to have to do this," Bishop Jenkins said. "But I have to do what God told me to do."

"No, you didn't, Bishop," one of the parishioners said. "You did not have to do that." The man picked up his overcoat and walked out of the service. He stopped before exiting the sanctuary. "And we ain't coming back until our pastor is back. Know that."

The bishop stood quietly as everyone in the church filed out quietly.

Church leaders and ministerial staff were fuming in the pastor's boardroom. No one was talking as they sat around the long table.

Two deacons paced behind those who were seated. Several ministers were breathing deeply and staring at nothing. Others seemed to be praying with their eyes closed and heads swaying. Rage and disbelief were everyone's close companions. Quentin sat quietly at the head of the table with pain, anger, disgust, and plots of revenge colliding in his mind.

"What was that?" Sister Brown asked.

"That was the bishop flexing his muscles," Quentin replied. "He doesn't want our churches to close, but *that* was ridiculous."

One of the leaders looked out the window. "Church must be over 'cause everyone is leaving."

"What a mess," Quentin said, shaking his head in disbelief. "What a mess."

After about ten minutes, Bishops Jenkins and Dillard walked into the boardroom with scowls on their faces.

Quentin's father looked at his son and commanded, "Pastor Dillard, in your office."

"I'm not sure I have an office, sir," Quentin said calmly without moving. "I believe I have been removed from my pastoral duties here." He looked at his father. "Did you have anything to do with this?"

There had been rumors floating around the church that Quentin had chosen to ignore because he knew church folks loved to gossip. People told him his father was trying to get the church back. But Quentin had let that, like the many other rumors and innuendos in the church, roll off his back. He knew his father was old, sick, and in no condition to take over a growing, diverse congregation.

"We will not discuss this in front of your staff," his father said, glaring at his son. "Please let's go into your office." Quentin's office was connected to the boardroom.

Quentin did not move.

"Young man, as the bishop emeritus of this church *and* your father, I request your presence in the pastor's office. Please," Cornell said with an authority he had not displayed in years.

Quentin slowly stood, staring at his father and Bishop Jenkins. He turned to his staff. "Y'all can go home. I'll be in touch with each of you. Pray for me and Greater Faith." He looked at his father and the bishop. "Let me straighten up the office."

While the church leaders and staff slowly exited the boardroom, Quentin walked through his office door.

When the room emptied, both bishops sat at the conference room table.

"You haven't told him about the slice yet?" Bishop Jenkins asked Cornell in a soft voice.

"I tried to tell him, but he didn't understand, and I don't know if he'd be willing to do it."

"This is how the bishops and *smart* pastors make our money. You know that," Bishop Jenkins said. "*You* certainly used it. There is no way any pastor can survive in the current gift structure. With the size of this church and the financial records I've seen, Quentin could be pulling in an additional $100,000 a year. And my part feeds my office. And you haven't told him? Well, where is the money going?"

"I've got everything under control," Cornell said. "And when I think he's ready, I'll show him the way."

"I've been short-changed these last three years not getting my slice from Greater Faith," Bishop Jenkins whispered. "You better tell him quick. But after today, we might have to execute Plan B. That's what you've wanted all the time anyway."

Quentin called the two men into his office. Bishop Jenkins sat behind the desk while Cornell took one of the three seats in the small office. The room was anchored by Quentin's large desk, and pictures of his family and his famed artwork covered the walls. Its three bookshelves were filled with several titles from his father's collection and books from Quentin's days in seminary. Quentin decided to stand.

"Quentin, I have known you all your life," Bishop Jenkins began. "And for the rest of your life, if you ever disrespect me like that, I'll have your church and your credentials, and you will never preach in the CFC again. Do you understand?"

Quentin took a few deep breaths. "This is what I understand, Bishop. You came into *my* church without giving me any prior notification. Then you flexed your muscles in front of my congregation and ordered me out of *my* pulpit. I don't care who you think you are—"

"Quentin!" his father yelled.

"No, Bishop Dillard. Please allow me to finish," Quentin said, turning to Bishop Jenkins. "You are nothing more than a figurehead in here. You do nothing for this church accept take our assessments every month, and I know that Greater Faith is one of your most profitable churches. Your bishops' board was too scared to give us directions when this pandemic started, and now you're gonna waltz in here and tell me I can't close the church when I have dozens of people in the hospital?"

"What does it look like if the church of Christ closes?" Bishop Jenkins asked calmly.

"It looks like we care for our people and we are doing all we can to protect them," Quentin replied. "You tell me what it looks like when you come here and tell me I can't take care of my people. I tell you what"—Quentin reached into his pocket, pulled out the keys, and tossed them toward the bishop— "you preach and keep the doors of the church open. I'm done. And I hope you and your board are ready to handle all the lawsuits coming your way."

Quentin began collecting his things. "Just calm down, son, and we can work this out," his father said in a softer tone. As Cornell peered at his son through smudged glasses, his eyes revealed a sadness that captured the moment.

"Maybe *you* can work it out," Bishop Jenkins said, each word wrapped in anger, "but all I see is an insubordinate pastor who believes he is bigger than the law."

Quentin stopped before exiting. "It is this county's law advising us to close the church. Power has caused you to lose your mind." He left the room and slammed the door of his office shut.

Bishop Jenkins was furious. He looked at Bishop Dillard. "OK, Cornell, like we agreed. I'll give you the church back, and you increase your payments to my episcopal office by 20 percent. That's just between you and me. Is that a deal?"

Bishop Dillard would not make eye contact with Bishop Jenkins. He said, "I know that is what we talked about, but let me think about it. The kid is doing a good job, and I don't know if I'm strong enough right now to take over Greater Faith."

Bishop Jenkins closed his eyes and rocked his head slowly from side to side. He put his hands together below his chin as he breathed deeply and coughed slightly. "You've got a choice. Convince your son to keep the church open and tell him about the slice and get an agreement and we're cool. If not, you can take over with our agreement or you can watch all this crumble and burn."

CHAPTER 5

CLOSING SHOWDOWN

Quentin turned off his cell phone during the drive home after the tumultuous church service and confrontation with Bishop Jenkins. Members of the congregation were calling and texting him with words of encouragement and frustration. His father called several times, and his mother sent him a rare text demanding that he contact her, but he didn't want to talk to anyone. He was livid and devastated. He seemed to flow in and out of consciousness, refusing to believe what had occurred.

Vanessa greeted him as he entered the house, but he held up his hand and shook his head as he made his way into his office. He felt like he could breathe for the first time as he sat at his desk in disbelief. Tears welled in his eyes and flowed down his face.

He finally broke down and sobbed. "God, I don't know what you're doing," he said. "But I'm gonna trust you. I need your strength to prevent me from doing something I'll regret."

Vanessa came into the office with a large glass of water. "It's gonna be all right, baby. We'll get through this." She touched him softly on his shoulder, and he gently placed his hand on hers. She began to cry. She wrapped her arms around him, and they wept together. The house phone rang, and the front doorbell buzzed, but they did not move. Their two daughters ran into the office.

"Momma, do you want me to answer the door?" asked Karlene, their oldest daughter at eight years old, as she stared at her weeping parents. "Did somebody die?" she asked.

Karlene was the observant, serious daughter. She rarely smiled but was very inquisitive and loved reading all types of books. She looked the most like her mother.

"No, babies. Just let it ring right now."

"Are y'all OK?" asked Kyla. She was six.

"We're just fine. Go downstairs and watch TV," Vanessa told them. "We'll be with you soon."

Kyla, the daddy's girl, stared at her father until he smiled. She was still missing a few teeth, but her smile always melted Quentin like butter in a hot skillet. Kyla was the playful one, always getting into trouble and talking herself into more trouble.

"It's OK, baby girl," he said. "We'll be OK. You two go downstairs."

"I wanna stay up here," Kyla said.

Vanessa stunned her with a laser look that spoke through the silence.

"OK, I guess we are going downstairs," Kyla said. "Come on, Leeny."

After the girls dashed out of the room, Quentin reached into one of his desk drawers, pulled out a handkerchief, and wiped his face. He found a small pack of Kleenex and gave them to Vanessa.

"Are we going to be just fine?" he asked.

"Without question," Vanessa replied confidently. "God is on our side. No matter what happened today, you are still the pastor of Greater Faith and the man God placed over that flock. You have been selected to lead us through this pandemic and all associated battles, including this one. I know you're hurt, but the battle is not over. And in the end, the battle is not yours; it's the Lord's."

Vanessa always had a way of bolstering Quentin's spirits. The COVID-19 crisis was not the first time the church had knocked them around, though it may have been the most powerful blow.

Vanessa knew Quentin was a resilient fighter who took pride in getting up from the canvas and continuing to throw blows.

"So if you're finished with your pity party," Vanessa said, "it's time to put a plan in place."

"I'm good," Quentin said softly. "Give me a little time to pray, and I'll let you know my next move."

"And don't forget to pray for the bishop *and* your father because they have lost their minds," Vanessa said as she left the room. "I love you, man of God. Be like Joshua. God is with you."

Quentin opened his Bible to the first chapter of Joshua, one of his favorite books. He always loved how God bathed Joshua with confidence by telling him to be bold and courageous and not afraid. Quentin slipped into his Joshua sandals as he read: "Do not be terrified; do not be discouraged, for the Lord your God will be with you wherever you go."

In this house, Quentin knew those words were meant for him. He prayed for the next ten minutes. Then he pulled out his notebook to devise a strategy to get back into his church and establish himself as a leader during the pandemic. The Holy Spirit flooded his mind with ideas. He was going to record a few videos, open Facebook, and Instagram pages, write an opinion piece for the local newspaper, and begin sending update emails to his congregation. His focus would be safety and a desire to love one's neighbors by keeping them safe. He smiled as the plan came together. *Thank you, Lord*, he said softly.

The phone continued to vibrate. Quentin rarely answered a call when the number was not in his phone. And there were several important calls that he chose not to answer. He wanted to clear his head and map out the plan. But the call from his mother altered his plans.

"Hey, Momma."

"Well, it's about time. This is my eighth call in the last hour, and I know you see my name on that crawler ID thing, and you better pick up for your momma."

"I just picked up. I had to turn my phone off with all the madness. But yours is the first and only call I'll answer."

"I know you're not picking up your father's calls."

"Not today or tomorrow," Quentin said. "He really pissed me off, and I can't believe he'd partner with Bishop Jenkins to take the church from me."

There was a pause before Quentin's mother continued. "I have called as sort of a peacemaker," she said, "because you need to talk to your father. Things went a little too far, and he knows that. He told me he didn't know what the bishop would do. But you need to know that he's changed since he got sick, and you took over the church. Sometimes I don't even know who he is."

"Be that as it may," Quentin replied, "he should have done something to stop Bishop Jenkins. Instead, he stood beside the bishop like a little puppy while the man kicked me out of my church."

"You gonna have to forgive your father," she said. "He's not perfect. If you gonna preach it, you gotta live it. So promise me you'll talk to your father."

Quentin did not respond.

"Did you hear me, boy?"

"Yes, Momma, I'll talk to *your* husband."

"You ain't slick," she snapped. "First, he's *your* father. Secondly, I want you to talk to him *today*. I know you're thinking, *I didn't say when I'd talk to him.*"

Quentin had to laugh because his mother knew him so well.

He hung up the phone but did not call his father immediately. That was going to take some time. Deep in his heart, he knew his father probably meant no harm. He was old-school. Of course, his father's generation never faced a global pandemic, but they did battle segregation and Jim Crow. Then the church was essential. They would never consider closing one of the few places Black people could go and find peace. *But this is different*, Quentin thought. There was no peace anywhere people gathered. Too many people were getting sick. *There comes a time when you have to do something you've never done before*, Quentin thought.

His phone vibrated again, and Quentin peeked at the caller ID. It was his old friend Marcel.

"What's up, man? I know you ain't calling me to give words of comfort."

"No, I'm not. I'm calling to see how you're planning to fight this. I think the bishop has lost his mind. Who does he think he is?"

"That doesn't matter right now," Quentin said. "I don't care what he said or what he did. I'm still the pastor of Greater Faith, and I'm putting something together to let the people know. I was hurt, but this is evidence that the love of money makes men do ridiculous things, in and outside the church."

"You think this was about money?" Marcel asked.

"I know this was about money," Quentin replied with a "no doubt" stamp in his voice. "If every church in the district closes, how is the bishop gonna get paid? We're the ones who not only pay his salary but support his entire staff. And our bishops live large."

"That's a shame, man. I was just calling to let you know I'm with you. And whatever you need, just holler."

"Thanks for calling bro. When the plan is finished, I'll let you know."

As soon as Quentin hung up the phone, the doorbell rang again. This must have been someone without much patience because it rang and rang. Quentin hesitated, but he knew Vanessa would not answer the door. He opened the doorbell app on his phone and saw his father and Bishop Jenkins standing outside. Quentin was not surprised. He knew this confrontation was going to take place. The doorbell rang again. Then there was a pounding on the door.

As he walked toward the front of the house, he could hear his father yelling, "You might as well come to the door because we ain't going nowhere."

Quentin stared at the closed door. "I'm going to call the police!" he yelled.

"I'm gonna call your mother," his father responded.

Quentin took a deep breath and opened the door. His father's eyes were as large as quarters. Sweat was beading on his forehead, despite the chilly afternoon.

"You all right, Pops?" Quentin asked.

"All right? No, I am not all right!" Cornell shouted, walking quickly through the doorway.

Bishop Jenkins stood stoically, awaiting an invitation. Quentin was overwhelmed with the urge to slam the door in the bishop's face, but he had been raised better.

"Come in, Bishop Jenkins."

The bishop nodded and strolled in like he was royalty. He had an air about him that screamed, *"I am better than you."* And the bishop's condescending smile made Quentin's stomach bubble. Quentin's father had gone into the kitchen to retrieve a glass of water. His heavy breathing made Quentin nervous.

"Pops, you need to sit down."

"I'm not going to sit down until we straighten out this mess," he said frantically.

"Well," Quentin said. "Why don't we all go into the dining room where we can sit and talk? Bishop, would you like some water?"

"No, but I would like some tea. Do you have Earl Grey?"

Quentin looked at him with a disgusting frown. "Earl Grey? I got Lipton."

"Well, if that's all you have. I'll take a cup with a little cream and a dab of honey."

Quentin had to bite his lip.

"Quentin," his father said. "Bishop Jenkins is a guest in your home."

"He was a guest in my church too, and he took it over!" Quentin exclaimed. "Has he come to take my house too?" He glared at Bishop Jenkins.

"I deserve that," the bishop said, coughing slightly. "Things got a little out of hand this morning, and I had no intention of taking your church. But when you came at me, I had to push back. I *am* your bishop."

"You didn't act like my bishop," Quentin said as Bishop Jenkins took off his overcoat and sat at the table. "You didn't act like someone concerned for me and the welfare of my congregation. To be truthful, you acted like a power-wielding tyrant."

Bishop Jenkins shook his head. "You are your father's son. He could never hold his tongue either."

"What do you mean by that?" Cornell asked.

"Cornell, you stayed in trouble even after you were a bishop because you wouldn't keep your mouth shut. You've got to know how to play the game."

"Well, what game were *you* playing today?" Quentin asked.

The bishop shifted in his seat. "This is no game, son. It is my responsibility to keep our churches thriving. I was merely carrying out my mission."

"That makes no sense, man," Quentin said.

"Quentin!" his father yelled.

"No, Pops. I am not going to let him come in here with some tired company line. What he did this morning had nothing to do with keeping the church thriving and everything to do with keeping the money flowing from our church to his pockets."

Bishop Jenkins cleared his throat and then smiled. "Is my tea coming?"

Quentin was trying to keep his cool. He was glad that his father was in the room.

"And I am sorry you have such a low opinion of your bishop and how your denomination does business," Jenkins said. "We are trying to do God's will, and we believe emphatically that the members of our churches should have a place to worship."

"Even if the place of worship is where people are getting sick?" Quentin asked as he stood up. "Even when everything we love to do like sing, hug each other, and fellowship are virus-spreading activities? This is like telling the people to go worship in a minefield but watch your step and don't forget to bring your offering."

"God will provide," Jenkins said sternly.

"Is that what you are telling the families of all the pastors and church leaders who are getting sick?" Quentin asked. "We know what God *can* do. The question is what *is* God doing now? Maybe we need to open our eyes to see God's new thing. And this should certainly not be about trying to keep our churches open so you can continue to get paid."

"This has nothing to do with me or whether I get paid or not. I'm on salary. I get paid no matter what." Bishop Jenkins said, obviously irritated. "I want to make sure *you* don't lose the church. I know you have a sizeable mortgage on your new campus. And if my sources are correct, some of the people with their hands in the pot are not what I consider traditional lenders." He flashed an eerie smile.

Quentin shook his head, acknowledging that the bishop knew more than he realized. "I thought you would congratulate me for using a Black-owned lender," Quentin said.

"I do like that. But that can go either way. Any Black-owned lender who can give you that much money has got to be one ruthless son of a gun."

"Bishop, we got this," Quentin responded calmly. "We can handle our mortgage to all our financial backers for at least six months if we don't get another dime. Plus, we're just closing the building; we're not closing the church."

"Will you still be making your payments to the episcopal office?" Jenkins asked.

"I thought this wasn't about *your* money," Quentin added.

Bishop Jenkins forced a smile. "I'm thinking about my staff and our work as a church nationally and worldwide."

Quentin moved toward the kitchen. "Did you want cream in that tea, or should I add some more—"

"Quentin Elisha," his father called out as Quentin left the room.

Bishop Jenkins began coughing loudly. "Bishop, are you sure you're all right?" Cornell asked. "You've been coughing all day."

"I'm fine, I'm fine," he said, clearing his throat again. "I've had this dry cough for a couple of days. I think it's allergies, and I just need a few sips of tea."

Quentin returned with the tea and plopped the cup and saucer in front of Bishop Jenkins. "Are you going to give me my church back?"

Bishop Jenkins tasted the tea and frowned. "I had planned to, but I don't like your attitude, young man. It's not *your* church. The church belongs to God. I'm going to put this up before a vote of the board. But prepare for a change. At the very least, you will be facing some disciplinary action."

"Oh, come on, Jeremiah," Cornell said. "Is this necessary? Greater Faith is one of your gold-standard churches, and you know that Quentin has done an outstanding job growing this church. Why would you do this?"

"Because I can," Jenkins said as he pushed the tea away. "That is repulsive. And so is Quentin's attitude. I will let you know when and if you will return to Greater Faith," he said to Quentin. "And while you are waiting for our decision, find some humility. It will help you avoid trouble."

Bishop Jenkins stood up. "Cornell, please take me to my hotel. I'm tired." He began to cough and wobble and had to lean on the table. He looked disoriented as he slowly sat down again.

Quentin went into the kitchen and got the digital thermometer. When he returned, he pointed it at the bishop's forehead, and his eyes pop open. "Sir, your temperature is 102.3. I think you should go to the hospital."

"That thing must be wrong," the bishop said, blinking, shaking his head, and reaching for his tea. "I don't feel that bad."

Quentin redid the test. It read 101.9. "Pops, he's got to go now."

Vanessa walked in. "If the bishop has to go to the hospital, Dad is not taking him. You have too many preexisting conditions," she said, looking at Cornell. "You probably shouldn't even be in the room with him."

"But I've been with him all day," Cornell said with a strange look on his face. "And we rode in the car here together."

"Bishop Jenkins, call your driver, and if you don't go to the hospital, I will call the police," Vanessa said sternly. She looked around the room at the three men, who looked lost. She quickly took control, as she was known to do.

"Dad, I'm calling your wife and telling her you must take the COVID-19 test tomorrow and be put in a fourteen-day quarantine," Vanessa said. "I will be watching you carefully. Now let's move, gentlemen."

Vanessa called Quentin's mother. "Mom, this is Vee. We're pretty sure Bishop Jenkins has the rona, and your husband has been with him all day. So, Dad has to take a test and go into a fourteen-day quarantine."

There was a long silence before Quentin's mother spoke. "Baby, ain't no way I can stay in the house with that man for fourteen straight days. I love him, you know that, but with his restless, gotta-go spirit, I'd probably kill him by day six."

"Can't you just stay in separate rooms?" Vanessa asked.

"This is when I wish we would have bought a bigger house. This one right here is not big enough for the two of us. Not for fourteen days."

"I'll be praying for you, but this is where we are," Vanessa said.

"All right. You send him home, and if I'm not here, tell him I'm at the Ritz Carlton downtown for the next two weeks. I want to save my marriage and keep from going to jail."

Vanessa got off the phone and walked back into the room with Quentin and her father-in-law.

"She told you she couldn't stay in the house with me for fourteen days, didn't she?" Cornell said with a laugh, wiping sweat from his forehead.

Vanessa bit her lip.

"It's OK. I get slightly out of control after a few days," Cornell said. "Quentin, remember that time I tried to jump off the cruise ship after three days of the ten-day cruise?"

"Yeah, we thought you lost your mind," Quentin recalled. "That was one time I wished you *were* a drinking man."

"So, what happened?" Vanessa asked.

"I calmed down and rode it out," Cornell said.

"In reality," Quentin added with a coy smile. "We started slipping melatonin and valerian root in his tea every night to knock him out."

"Is that why I slept so well? That was mighty sneaky," Cornell said with a smile. "Thank you."

Vanessa was able to find someone to take Bishop Jenkins to the hospital. It took the bishop quite a while to gather the strength to make it to the waiting vehicle. His cough was getting worse, and he was obviously weak as he forced himself into the large SUV and slumped in the seat. Vanessa told the driver to keep his mask on and his window open despite the cold weather.

Quentin was anxious to hear from the board of bishops, but after a week, he had not received any communications. He asked his father what was going on, but Cornell told him he was not allowed to participate in any meetings because they involved his son. After ten days, Quentin called the episcopal office.

"Hello, this is Thelma Hudson, executive secretary of the southeast episcopal region."

"Hello, this is Rev. Quentin Dillard. I am calling about a decision of the board of bishops concerning my church, Greater Faith Temple of Praise."

"Oh, I know who you are. You're Bishop Dillard's son," Thelma said.

"Yes, I am. I'm wondering if a decision has been made about my status?"

"How is your father doing?" she asked. "You tell him you talked to me. I'm Thelma. It has been far too long since he visited the office."

Quentin paused. "I will let my father know. Now, about the board of bishops."

"Doesn't your father know?" Thelma asked. "He is such an intelligent and intellectual man."

"No, he doesn't know," Quentin said, a bit disturbed at the direction of the conversation. "He would not be able to vote on any decision because I'm his son."

"Well, the board is having problems meeting with all this digital stuff. Half the bishops think Zoom is a song by Lionel Ritchie." She laughed. "I believe they have all received a document from Bishop Jenkins, but he's sick, and I was told that half the things he wrote were nonsensical. I know you made him angry, and he is recommending that ... Oh, I can't tell you that."

"I think you can tell me. After all, it is my future."

"But it's not my place, and I'm trying to keep my job. They're laying off all kinds of people around here, and COVID-19 is having a devastating economic effect here."

"You're telling me there hasn't been a decision."

"I thought I told you that," Thelma said matter-of-factly. "Look, we have three bishops who don't have computers *or* smartphones. Ain't nothing worse than a flip-phone bishop. Anyway, it may take a while before anything happens, especially with all this sickness. Is your father doing OK?"

Quentin was beyond frustrated. "Look, Sister Thelma, I'm just trying to get some information."

"We don't have anything for you. You will be notified of the board's decision if and when the bishops meet."

"What am I supposed to do until then?"

"Be the pastor, I guess."

"Sister Thelma, I am so confused."

"Look, young man, do what you gotta do. I ain't seen a bishop in almost three months. Ain't no telling when these bishops are gonna get together again. We're just hoping we can have a meeting before we have another funeral. I gotta go, but please tell your dear father Sister T said hello. He'll know who you're talking about."

Quentin hung up with a strange feeling in his stomach. He decided to move forward as the fully empowered pastor of Greater Faith. He wondered why Bishop Jenkins did what he did and what was up with Sister Thelma and his father, but he had to focus on letting his congregation know he was still their pastor.

CHAPTER 6

A DOUBLE BLESSING

Quentin was pulled from a short sleep when his phone vibrated at 4:30 a.m. In most cases, he did not answer his phone until after 9:00 a.m., giving him time to wake up, clean up, and do his morning devotional. However, this morning the Holy Spirit woke him and allowed him to hear his phone vibrating from across the bedroom.

"Hello. This is Pastor Q," he said, tiptoeing and whispering, hoping not to wake Vanessa.

"Pastor, I am so sorry to call you at this time, but we are in desperate need of prayer."

Quentin did not immediately recognize the male voice, but he sensed desperation wrapped in an African accent. "Who is this, and what's going on?" he asked, trying to clear the cobwebs from his mind.

"Oh, oh, I am so sorry, sir. This is Adembe, and Shalela has got it," the man said in a rhythmic staccato draped in sadness and fear. "She appears to be gravely ill. They are saying the babies might not make it."

Quentin still could not identify the caller. "Who is this?" he asked.

"This is Adembe Yeboah. Remember, you prayed for us to have children, and Shalela finally got pregnant with twins."

That turned the light on. "Oh, Adembe, I got you. Now, what's going on?"

"Shalela's got it, Pastor."

"She's got what?"

"She's got the coronavirus, and it's bad. She's in the hospital, and they are saying she might not make it. They want to take the babies, but they are only twenty-six weeks, and Shalela wants them to grow. But she can hardly breathe. She's weak. Oh my, Pastor. There is a chance they could all die."

Quentin shifted into full pastor mode. "No one is going to die, Adembe." He began to pray. "Father in the powerful and potent name of Jesus …" Quentin called on God to heal Shalela, save the babies, and calm Adembe's troubled spirit.

"Where are you, Adembe?"

"I am at home. I am going batty in here, but they will not let me in the hospital."

"Text me your address. I'm on my way."

Quentin had known Adembe and Shalela for about three years. They came to the church and joined during their first visit. They were both from Ghana and had relocated to the States for a better life. They were a jovial couple who immediately became a part of several ministries in the church. After about six months, they had requested a meeting. It turned out that they had been trying to have children but were unsuccessful. It was a second marriage for them both, and Shalela hoped that her inability to become pregnant was unrelated to her age. At forty-two, she was spry, invigorated, and anxious to become a mother.

She worked part-time at the church's childcare center, using her degree in early childhood education to infuse new programs in the school. Adembe was a licensed plumber and carpenter who worked with several large construction companies and also did work on the side. He almost had a full-time job working for members of the church. Six weeks after meeting with the pastor, Shalela had discovered she was pregnant with twins.

Adembe welcomed Quentin at the door with a huge hug. Quentin immediately knew Adembe had little regard for COVID-19 protocol. Maskless, Adembe, a tall, thin man with a hug that could take one's breath away, invited Quentin inside. Adembe had always seemed serious, with a sense of humor that did not sync with American culture. He spoke with a deep, pounding monotone laced with an African rhythmic flow that sometimes made him difficult to understand.

The small apartment was dimly lit, and an assortment of strange fragrances spiraling from candles and incense danced in Quentin's nose. Adembe looked nervous and tired and was wearing clothes that had not been ironed. His bloodshot eyes told Quentin that sleep was currently not Adembe's friend.

"Adembe, it looks like you need some rest."

"How can I rest, Pastor?" he said in a voice clothed with hopelessness. He looked like a man without any answers. "My wife is in the hospital. She is six months pregnant with twins. She is very, very sick, and I cannot visit her. She can only say a few words to me on the phone. The doctor talks to me, but I do not understand her medical mumbo jumbo. I just know it is bad, and I feel like I am losing my mind. I have not slept in two days. I do not know what to do."

Quentin could feel the frustration oozing from each of Adembe's words. "Please sit down, Adembe," he said. "Pacing the floor and thinking the worst is not going to help. I am going to pray with you and be with you. And know that God is with Shalela. Our God will take care of her."

Adembe kept pacing, taking deep breaths, and rubbing his hands through his uncombed Afro-gone-wild hair.

"Adembe, please sit down," Quentin said, raising his voice slightly.

Adembe looked at Quentin like he had just realized his pastor was in the room.

"All right, Pastor, I'll try, but my mind is swimming. Why can

I not be with my wife?" he asked as he sat on the edge of a worn light blue sofa.

"It's this virus. The coronavirus," Quentin said. "They aren't letting anyone in the hospital because there are too many sick people, and this virus is highly contagious."

"That makes no sense. There are always sick people in the hospital!" Adembe shouted. "I need to be there with my wife and my babies. We have waited so long for this. What am I to do?" He popped up and began pacing again.

"You will sit down and tell me how all this happened. Please, sit down."

Adembe sat down and stared into space. "Shalela works with children, you know. She goes to different centers and works with children with mental troubles. About two months ago, she came home with a cough. We did not think anything of it. We thought it was allergies, but it got worse."

"Did you go to the hospital?"

"Of course, we did. She was pregnant for the first time, and we were not going to take any chances. The doctors did not know what was wrong with her, and this virus had not materialized like it is today. They sent her home and told her to rest. She felt better and went back to work in a few days."

"Was she acting differently?" Quentin asked.

"Yeah, yeah. She was always tired and did not want to eat." Adembe paused and shook his head. "And she complained that her food tasted funny. But we thought it was the pregnancy. My God, if we only would have known."

"There's no way you could have known," Quentin said.

"After a while, it got so bad that she couldn't work anymore," Adembe recalled. "And the cough came back, and she had a fever. She was not looking well, and I did not want her to leave the bed. I finally took her to the hospital, and corona was in full force by that time. All she would tell me is that I had to take care of the babies."

"What was the doctor saying about the pregnancy?"

"To be truthful, Pastor, once she told me that Shalela had the virus, I could not comprehend a thing. All I was doing was praying."

"Is she at Adventist or St. Anthony's Hospital?"

"She is at Adventist."

"That's good, that's good," Quentin said.

"No, Pastor, it is not good that my wife is in the hospital," Adembe countered.

"No, no. It is good that she is at Adventist," Quentin explained. "I know someone there who might be able to help us. Sister Barbara is a church member and a nursing supervisor at Adventist. Let me make a call."

Quentin had to leave a message for Barbara Courtney, but his immediate concern was Adembe. Quentin made tea and prayed with him. After talking and praying, they both fell asleep. Quentin was awakened hours later by his vibrating phone and the rising sun.

"This is Pastor Q."

"This is Sister Barbara, Pastor. I got your message this morning and checked on Shalela. I can't give you information because she is a patient and—"

"Come on, Sister Barbara, we've done this too many times," Quentin said.

There was a long silence. "It's not good, Pastor. She is very sick, and to be truthful, the doctors don't know if she's going to make it. She can't take stronger medicine because she's pregnant. She's on and off the ventilator, her blood pressure is flying, and there is fear that the babies won't survive."

This was not the news Quentin wanted to hear. He looked at Adembe, who was sleeping soundly, and didn't know what to do.

"What are the next steps?" Quentin asked.

"You need to pray because this is definitely in God's hands," Barbara said. "The doctors are going to have to make the decision soon to take the babies. Whenever she wakes up, she tells the attending nurses to keep the babies in her as long as possible. I am standing near the room, and everyone who goes in there comes out crying."

"Can we do the thing?" Quentin asked.

"I don't know, Pastor. That's kinda risky."

"I am here with her husband, and he is not doing well. We at least need to try."

Barbara took a deep breath. "OK, but if this backfires, I'll be living in your house."

Quentin walked to the front window and parted the drapes. He marveled at the various hues as the sun rose slowly above the eastern hills. It was a beautiful sight that did not seem possible after hearing the news about Shalela and the unborn babies. The array of colors, the calmness of the hour, and the emerging sunshine gave Quentin hope. He began to pray.

"Lord, I often ask my people, 'Whose report do you believe?' And I encourage them only to believe the report of the Lord. So now it is time to put those words into action. I have heard what the doctors have said. I understand that the prognosis is dim, so I have come to you. In your Word, there are many stories about hopeless situations that were turned around by faith. In my life, I have experienced your power to turn the impossible to possible. Lord, I bring you Shalela Yeboah and ask for a miracle. While the doctors determine who can be saved, I am asking that you touch and protect everyone involved, the mom and the babies. I come by faith, knowing that you are able. I come in faith believing in the might of your healing power, Lord."

Tears began to roll down Quentin's face.

"Lord, please. Touch the lives of this family, and I know they will give you all the glory, honor, and praise. They were obedient, calling on the elders of the church. Now, God, do what you do. I know you to be a miracle-working God. I am anxious to see your works."

Quentin's phone vibrated, which was unusual, so early in the morning. Usually during such intense communication with God, he would not answer, but the Holy Spirit prompted him.

It was Barbara.

"Hello?"

"Pastor, they're going to take the babies. Shalela's blood pressure is extremely unstable, and her breathing is so sporadic that they don't think she is going to make it."

"We're moving." He disconnected the call. "In your hands, Lord. Thank you. Amen."

Quentin woke Adembe and told him they needed to head to the hospital.

"But they will not let us in," Adembe insisted, fighting to wake up.

"Let me worry about that," said Quentin while composing a text message. It was a thirty-minute ride that he needed to make in twenty minutes. There was no time to waste. "Let's roll."

Adembe was a nervous wreck during the drive. "I do not understand, Pastor. Why must we go to the hospital and stand outside? I have tried for days to get in. I even considered injuring myself so that I could at least get through the doors."

"You don't have to do that. We'll get in," Quentin insisted.

"Pastor, you are a great man of faith."

Adembe's phone rang. "Yes." He listened. "Oh my, oh my. I am on my way. I know I can't get in, but I must be there. Take care of my wife, and please save the babies."

His breathing was pronounced when he hung up the phone. "They have to take the babies, and everyone is in danger of dying. Oh God, this cannot be happening."

"Adembe, have faith. God is on our side," Quentin said as he sped toward the hospital.

"God has been on our side, and my wife and babies are dying," Adembe said as he searched for a station on the radio.

Quentin looked as Adembe started mouthing the words to Blake Shelton's "Nobody But You."

"You listen to country music? Really?" Quentin asked.

"It relaxes me," Adembe said. "I love the words and the stories. *I don't want to dream without you. I want to wake up next to you.*"

Adembe was singing his heart out, though slightly off-key. Quentin was amazed.

"So tell me this. How did a brother from Ghana get into country music?"

Adembe laughed softly. "When we first moved to this country, we stayed with Shalela's relatives in Kentucky, and that was the only music they played. I thought *all* Black people in America listened to country music. Then we went to a Darius Rucker concert and were hooked."

"You mean Shalela likes country music too?"

"She loves it. But she is into Lee Brie and Miranda Lambert."

"All righty then," Quentin said, totally in shock. "Have you ever listened to R&B?"

"Yeah, they can sing, but the stories are no good. *Looking in your eyes now, if I had to die now, I don't wanna love nobody but you.*"

"Is your love for country music the reason neither you nor your wife joined any of the choirs?"

"I didn't join because I can't sing," Adembe said honestly. "I'm as flat as a skillet, but that don't matter with country music. Listen to this. Blake can't sing a lick, but he's got all kinds of hits."

"Can Shalela sing?"

"Can't find a note with a searchlight. Are we close to the hospital? I have never come this way," Adembe said.

"We're just a couple minutes out," said Quentin, speeding through the backroads.

"I still do not know why we have come all this way if we cannot get inside."

Quentin smiled. "We have come all this way to renew your faith and show you that God can do miracles."

Quentin pulled into the parking lot, sent a short text, and grabbed his blue surgical hat and blue mask. He handed Adembe a baseball cap from the back seat. Adembe looked at the cap and frowned.

"I do not support American sports teams," Adembe said.

"Just take the cap and pull it down over your eyes."

"If I pull it over my eyes, I will not be able to see."

"Do like this," Quentin said, showing him how low to pull the cap. "Now, I need you to follow my lead. And don't say anything. You got that?"

"Why are you wearing a shower cap?" Adembe asked.

"This is a surgeon's cap, and we have one for you inside."

"I am not a surgeon, and that head covering is ugly."

Quentin and Adembe, both masked, walked quickly to the side door of the hospital.

"But the main entrance is around the corner," Adembe roared, pointing toward the front of the hospital.

Quentin gave him a laser glare.

"I am to say nothing," Adembe said. "I understand."

Quentin knocked on the door, and security guard Shelton Fuller, a member of Greater Faith, opened it.

"Brother Shelton," Quentin said, pounding fists with the guard. "Thank you so much."

Quentin and Adembe moved quickly inside.

"Pastor Q, I could lose my job for this," Shelton said.

"Brother Shelton, we've done this before. We're good. Plus, God is on our side. You will not lose your job. You have the other cap and mask?"

"You didn't tell me you were bringing somebody. What is Adembe doing here?" Shelton asked.

"Just take us to the employee elevator," Quentin instructed. "We've got to get to the fifth floor. You got those badges?"

Shelton rolled his eyes, reached into his jacket pocket, and pulled out two unofficial hospital badges. "Guard these with your life," Shelton said.

"Pastor, my wife is on the third floor," Adembe announced.

"His wife?" Shelton asked. "Pastor, what's going on? We've done this before, but it's only been you coming to pray for somebody who was dying."

Quentin glared at Adembe.

"I am to say nothing," Adembe said stoically, staring straight ahead.

Quentin took Shelton to the side. Shelton was one of the leaders of the men's ministry at Greater Faith. Quentin explained the situation concerning Adembe's wife and the twins.

"This brother wants to be with his wife," Quentin explained. "We cannot deny him that."

"You right. You right," Shelton agreed. "I know you prayed about this."

"You know I did," Quentin replied.

"Then let's go," Shelton said.

They quickly moved down the hallway like they were spies in a *Mission Impossible* movie. Shelton had them hide in doorways and behind partitions as they made their way to the employee elevator. He gave the signal, and they ran through the doors.

"Where are all the nurses and attendants?" Quentin asked.

"Everyone has been pulled downstairs to deal with the COVID overflow. It's chaos down there, and all the other departments are operating with less than skeleton crews."

"Why are we going to the fifth floor?" Adembe asked.

Quentin could not believe Adembe was still talking. He held up his hand, and Adembe dropped his head.

"I know, I know. I am to say nothing."

"Don't even say that," Quentin snapped. "Nothing means nothing."

The elevator stopped, and the door opened on the fifth floor. Shelton held up his hand, indicating they should not move. Two doctors and a nurse rushed by.

"Stay close to me," Shelton whispered.

They made three quick turns and slipped through a set of double doors, which Shelton unlocked by swiping his card. They passed a large empty waiting room that would typically be filled with people waiting for loved ones to come out of surgery. Four televisions on the walls showed the morning news, but no one was watching. Shelton turned quickly and waved his hands like he was dribbling a basketball. Quentin knew that meant to get low. Adembe was clueless, looking around with his eyes open wide.

"Why is it so empty?" Adembe asked. "Is this not a good hospital?"

Quentin grabbed him by his belt and pulled him down. A nurse and an attendant walked by, reading a chart.

"It's the virus. Now hush," Quentin whispered.

"Why did you pull me like that?" Adembe asked loudly.

Shelton whirled around with his finger over his mouth, indicating that they should be quiet. He led them to a small waiting area with a bed, one small chair, and lots of lights and containers filled with liquids on the walls. Shelton pulled the drapes so they could not be seen.

"I'll be right back," Shelton said softly. "Do not leave this area, and *please* do not talk louder than a whisper." He looked at Adembe before leaving. "That means you."

"What are we doing here? Adembe asked. "Where is my wife?"

Quentin realized Adembe didn't grasp the severity of the situation. "Adembe, I need you to listen to me," he said with an authoritative whisper. "We are *not* supposed to be in here. If we get caught, we will probably go to jail, and you will not see your wife or your babies. Several people who are helping us will lose their jobs if we get caught. So please, be quiet. Say nothing. Silence, please," Quentin said with emphasis. "We will see your wife when the coast is clear."

"We are not near the water," Adembe responded with certainty.

"What?" Quentin asked.

"We are not near the water," Adembe repeated.

Quentin was confused. "What are you talking about?"

"You said we would see my wife when the coast is clear. But we are not near the coast, and we are not near any water."

Quentin shook his head. "OK. We just ain't gonna say another word until this is over."

After a few minutes, the curtain was pulled back quickly, taking Quentin's breath away. It was Barbara.

"Is Shalela here?" Quentin asked.

Barbara shook her head and pulled the curtain closed behind her. "She's down the hallway."

Adembe perked up and began to move. "Where is she?" he asked.

Quentin quickly stood in front of him, mask to mask. "I have told you that you have to follow directions, or we will get kicked out of here. Now calm yourself and let Sister Barbara direct us."

Adembe stopped his charge.

"What's the plan?" Quentin asked.

"She's due for surgery in about an hour," Barbara whispered. "They have her resting quietly, but she's not doing well." She looked at the pastor, pulled him away from Adembe, and whispered, "They don't think she's going to make it, but we'll try to save the babies."

Adembe started moving again. "I must see her," he said.

Quentin stepped in front of him again. "Adembe, if you don't calm down, you will be a future patient here because I'm gonna knock you into next week. Do you understand?"

Adembe, breathing deeply, gave an agreeing nod.

"Go ahead, Sister Barbara," Quentin said.

"When the doctors leave in a few minutes, I'll come back and get you, but you can only stay for a few minutes," she said. "Then we gotta get you outta here. I'll be back when the coast is clear."

"We are not near the water," Adembe called out to her.

"Sit down, Adembe, please. It will only be a few more minutes," said Quentin, who feared this journey may have been a mistake.

In the last two months, as the COVID hospitalizations increased, Quentin had slipped into the hospital at least three times with the help of Shelton and Barbara. But he had never gone to the presurgical waiting area or brought anyone with him. For Quentin, this was like a game of hide-and-seek, and he realized Adembe probably had not played such games in Ghana.

While waiting, Quentin sent a text to his prayer warrior group: *Time to pray. Sister Shalela is in crisis.*

After a minute, he received a text from his wife: *You didn't sneak into the hospital again, did you?*

He chose not to respond.

A few seconds later, another text from his wife came in: *Your message should have said you are in crisis.*

Just as he prepared a response, Barbara pulled back the curtain.

"Let's go. Move quickly," she whispered.

They scurried down the hall, passing a series of small patient waiting areas with curtains closed. She guided them into a corner room where Shalela lay with her eyes closed. An oxygen tube was in her nose, and several tubes were attached to her arm. Quentin was shocked when he saw her thin face. It looked like she had not eaten in weeks and her hair had not been combed in days. Adembe approached the bed and began to cry.

"My Lela." He took her hand and touched her cheek softly. He kissed her forehead, and as a tear touched her face, she struggled to open her eyes.

"Dembe, Dembe is it you?" she asked softly. "Am I dreaming?"

"I am here," Adembe replied, tears flowing. "It is going to be OK."

She closed her eyes and tried to breathe. "Please take care of the babies," she whispered. "Love them and tell them about their mother." She began to cough.

"I will let you tell them," Adembe said. "God will not take you home today. Pastor, we need you to pray."

Quentin wiped tears from his eyes. "I've been praying the entire time." He looked Shalela in the eye and could see she was tired and hurting. "Know by faith that God is with you and your babies," he said. "And soon, you will all leave this hospital ... alive."

Quentin prayed for the next few minutes. He could feel the presence of God in that space. He had never prayed, cried, and whispered at the same time. He was adamant about calling on power in the name of Jesus. He felt like he was going to pass out, but he continued to call on Jesus's name. As he prayed, his spirit was being transported to another dimension. He was wrapped in the power of the Holy Spirit. Then he heard the words: *She will live and not die and proclaim what the Lord has done.*

Barbara returned. "We've got to go. Others will be coming soon. My goodness it's hot in here."

"I will not leave," Adembe proclaimed.

"Adembe, you won't do your wife or your two beautiful babies any good in jail," Quentin said, reaching out to touch Adembe's shoulder. "God says we are good, so let's go."

"I will not leave her," he said firmly.

"We've got to go," Barbara insisted.

"Adembe, you are not God," Quentin said forcefully, wiping sweat from his forehead and tears from his eyes. "It is God who said *He* would never leave us. So she is in good hands, God's hands. We, on the other hand, need to get out of here. But I promise you will see your wife and babies soon."

"Go, Dembe, go," Shalela said softly. "And care for the babies."

"I will go, but I will care for you all. That is my promise." He kissed his wife on the forehead and followed Barbara and the pastor.

They passed several hospital personnel in the hallway but did not stop or turn around. Shelton was outside the waiting area doors. They made it to the employee elevator and got in with other hospital personnel.

"Shelton, did you catch more people sneaking in here?" one of the nurses asked.

He rolled his eyes. "I sure did. They think they're slick, but I got'em, and they gotta go."

"Where do they get these fake badges? They must be selling them on the street. You need to take their asses to jail," another nurse said. "They probably brought the rona up in here."

The elevator door opened, and Shelton grabbed Quentin and Adembe and led them out. "I got this. Y'all be safe."

When the elevator doors closed, Shelton released a sigh of relief. "That was close," he said. "Come on down here. I'm gonna hide you in the chapel until we get word on the babies. I'll tell Sister Barbara where you are, and she'll give you the news. Do not leave this room. You'll be safe here."

Adembe began to pace. "I should have stayed with her," he said. "I should be at her side."

"There's nothing you could do," Quentin said. "We just need to pray."

Quentin walked to the altar in front of the small chapel. The room was dimly lit, with several electric candles providing most of the light. Soft music was playing. He knelt at the altar, and Adembe joined him. They prayed for about five minutes. Then Quentin got up and went to the front pew. Adembe stayed at the altar. After about ten minutes, Quentin fell asleep.

"Pastor, Pastor," were the words that jarred Quentin from sleep. He did not know how long he had been out, but he knew he had been tired; the lack of sleep and the prayers had drained him. He looked up to see Barbara. Adembe was asleep on another pew.

"Pastor, the babies have arrived."

Adembe woke up slowly. When Quentin looked at his watch, he realized they had slept for more than an hour.

"The babies are here?" Adembe asked, standing slowly.

"Yes," Barbara said. "They are small, about two and a half pounds each, but you have two beautiful baby girls, and they're going to make it."

There was a long silence as Adembe seemed to look through

Barbara. "And my Lela?" he asked, forcing the words out of his mouth while bracing for the worst.

"She is a fighter, and God was fighting with her," Sister Barbara said.

There was another pause as Adembe closed his eyes and took a deep breath. "Did she win the fight?" he asked softly, tears welling in his eyes.

"It's a miracle. It's truly a miracle," Barbara said, wiping her eyes and shaking her head in disbelief. "She's still in critical condition, which is more than any of the doctors expected." Barbara's mind was locked in bewilderment. "She shouldn't be here. I'm telling you, there's no way she should be here. She is so weak, she has the virus, she can hardly breathe, and she had to undergo a difficult surgery with twins. My God, she is a miracle."

Adembe started crying. "Are you telling me my wife and my babies live?"

"Somehow," Barbara said, wiping tears from her eyes. "Yes, they are alive. God is truly a gracious God."

Adembe lifted both his hands into the air. "Thank you, Lord. Oh, God, I give you my thanks. Thank you, thank you, thank you." He hugged Barbara, and they cried together.

Tears cascaded down Quentin's face as he gave God praise. Again, Quentin heard the words: *She will live and not die and proclaim what the Lord has done.*

Over the next few days, Quentin worked with the Adventist Hospital chaplain and the hospital administration to allow Adembe to visit his wife and babies. Shalela was making steady progress and had been upgraded to stable condition. She was eating, sitting up in the bed, and able to see her babies from a distance because they were in incubators. Adembe was on cloud nine when he was able to walk through the front doors of the hospital with his pastor.

"No more clearing the coast, Pastor. God is awfully good."

Quentin reminded Adembe that he could not tell anyone he

had been in the hospital before the birth of his daughters, Faith and Miracle.

"I am to say nothing," Adembe said with a wide smile.

After they visited his wife, Adembe stopped Quentin in the hallway. "Pastor, I never got the opportunity to thank you. You took a great chance to take me into the hospital to see my Lela, and I thank you from the bottom of my heart. And I believe your prayers saved her and my babies. I had never seen anyone pray, cry, tremble and sweat at the same time. And there was a light around you, my God. That was awesome."

"That was God, Adembe," Quentin said. "It was the power of the Holy Spirit, and I just believed God did not take us that far to let us down. Now we can testify to the greatness of our Lord."

CHAPTER 7

———◆———

THE LOVE OF MONEY

L ife did not get easier for Quentin after the miracle at Adventist Hospital. People in and around the church continued to get sick. Attendance was dwindling in those churches that continued having live worship services on Sunday mornings. And Greater Faith was struggling, particularly in the embryonic stages of the virus.

The initial shift to live streaming was difficult with little updated technology, weak internet signals in the church, and a lack of technical support. The new online platform was not without mass confusion and a series of glitches. Zoom was in and out, Facebook Live struggled, and many members could not figure out how to connect.

One of the strengths of Greater Faith was its high-praise and energetic worship services, which could not be duplicated online. Quentin tried to adjust to preaching from home and then in an empty sanctuary, but he was not accustomed to delivering the word with no feedback or energy from the congregation. Becoming an internet church presented a learning curve that Quentin found challenging. He read books and watched endless videos on YouTube to learn how to handle this shift to doing church in a digital environment, but nothing eased the feeling that he was falling short of the mark.

After several weeks, a few ministries decided to reorganize to help a struggling community during the pandemic. Despite being unable to meet at the church, many church leaders learned how to operate Zoom to get the ministries up and running again. The church began to host monthly food giveaways, distributing tons of free fruits, vegetables, canned goods, boxed food, and meat to those in need. The revitalized clothing ministry collected and distributed clothes to the homeless and the less fortunate. Though the pastor or members of the Reach Out and Touch ministry could not visit the sick, they made sure to call the church's sick and shut-ins every month. The Health and Welfare ministry sponsored free COVID-19 tests, flu shots, and blood pressure screenings for the community.

In addition, Bible study and Sunday school started online. Within a few months, taking advantage of connections with county officials and programs, Greater Faith had a more prominent presence in the community than before the virus. Despite the return to working in the community, Quentin was being pressed to suspend all ministry activities.

"Pastor Q, we've got to cut back on all this ministry work," said Marcel. "We're doing good things. I know we are supposed to be helping people. But we're not getting the money we used to. These ministries are draining our resources."

"We can't stop doing ministry," Quentin insisted. "That's what we're here to do. Think about it: we can still help people, feed people, and clothe people even though our building is closed. That's awesome, and that says something about the church."

"No, Pastor. That's costly, and it says the church may soon be broke," Marcel responded. "I know you like us in the community, and that's probably what we need to be doing, but maybe we can say that we can't be out there because of the dangers of the virus."

"But people are still in need, Marcel. I want the people who are sending in their tithes and offerings to see that we are still about being the church and helping folks in these difficult times. If we stop serving, they'll stop giving. God will make a way. We follow all the county safety protocols during our ministry activities: everyone is wearing a mask, we do our best to social distance, and if I wash my hands anymore, I might be able to see my bones. I believe our testimony will be how we continue to serve the community, increasing our service in the middle of this pandemic. We *must* continue doing good. We may need to change how we spend our resources, but the ministry work must continue."

Marcel forwarded Quentin a copy of the latest finance report, which did not look good. With the utilities, mortgage, salaries, and ministry activities, the accounts were emptying quickly. To slow the drain, Marcel worked with the bank to negotiate a deal for the bank's portion of the mortgage, suspending payments for four months. The financier that held the second on the loan, Community Cares Banking Services, LLC (CCBS), a locally owned minority business, was not as generous.

Quentin met with Reggie Bliss, who had brought CCBS to the table. Reggie, a member of the church's finance committee, specialized in finding and tracking outside funding sources. He was being pressured because the church was several months late with its second mortgage payment. Reggie and Quentin had been friends since high school. The only reason Reggie was a part of any church was because of his long-time relationship with Quentin.

"Look, Reggie, we don't have the money to pay the CCBS this month," Quentin said. "Churches across the country are falling on rough times during this pandemic."

"I know the situation, Q, but Mr. Alonzo don't care. He wants his money."

Alonzo Johnson was the founder and CEO of CCBS.

"I know we can find the money somewhere. Things aren't that bad," Reggie said.

"We don't have it. Or let me put it another way," Quentin reasoned. "We can't spare it. We must prioritize our transactions, and I am not sure the second mortgage is on the top of my list."

"If you don't put it on the top, things could get ugly," Reggie said.

"He's got to be reasonable," Quentin countered. "We've been on time for years, but who could have predicted a global pandemic that is crushing churches and businesses all over the world? Banks and all other lending institutions are doing something to help."

"This ain't about what's happening all over the world or what other banks are doing," Reggie said. "It's about our agreement to pay CCBS four Gs every month. That's all this is. And the penalty is a problem."

"Maybe he can just charge us a higher interest rate like the money lenders do. And give us a few months to get back on our feet."

"Oh, he's gonna charge higher interest, but that's only the beginning."

Reggie seemed uncomfortable during this conversation. "Mr. Alonzo is an old-school gangster. He don't care if you're a pastor. He wouldn't care if you were the pope or Mary the mother of Jesus. If you aren't paying him, he tends to take drastic measures to get his money."

"What's he gonna do, bust my knees?" Quentin said, laughing. Reggie did not laugh or smile. "Are you serious? This dude would resort to violence?"

Reggie was wringing his hands. "Q, I'm so sorry to get you involved with this guy. I didn't realize how vicious he really was. He's a smooth talker, but I've heard he's certifiable."

"Why didn't you tell me he was a gangster when we made the deal?"

"It didn't matter then," Reggie replied. "Money was flowing like the Mississippi, and we had all the cash we needed to pay him. He had a minority-owned lending institution, which is hard to find, and I know that is what you wanted. *And* we were so close to making your dream happen. But now…"

"Let me talk to him," Quentin said bluntly.

"Naw, you don't want to talk to him."

"Come on, Reggie. Set up a meeting, face-to-face. If he's gonna take me out, he can at least look me in the eye and hear my case."

"I don't think you want to do that."

"Yeah, I do. Set it up, and I'll take my chances. And the dream is still alive. Don't forget that."

Reggie arranged a meeting for Quentin at Johnson's home. Quentin decided to do a deep dive into his lender's background, something he should have done before agreeing to the loan. Johnson had grown up in the neighborhood near the old church. There was not a lot of information online about how Johnson got his money. He had established several check-cashing outlets in low-income neighborhoods about fifteen years earlier. He specialized in payday lending and high-interest, short-term loans. His business continued to grow until he had the funds to make larger loans, allowing him to set up the CCBS.

But things got ugly when people or businesses couldn't pay, which frequently happened in the neighborhoods he served. Reports indicated the initial friendly customer service evolved into vicious threats, personal property damage, and escalating interest rates. Johnson had developed a reputation for *always* getting his money, earning the name Jack-You-Up Johnson.

Reggie had initially contacted Johnson's organization because the church needed an additional million dollars to close the deal on the new property, which was comprised of a five-hundred-seat sanctuary with a coffee shop, library, bookstore, classrooms, a large childcare facility, and a recreation hall with basketball courts and a small fitness center. It had been a dream come true for Quentin. Local banks had approved a four-million-dollar loan, but Quentin had wanted to purchase the entire campus, which required additional funds. Quentin had also been interested in CCBS because of the opportunity to work with a minority lending institution with community roots.

Quentin's father had thought purchasing the new church was over the top. "Son, we're just a small Black church; we're not a community center."

"But why not, Pops? Why can't we be all things for all people?" Quentin had asked. "I believe the more services we provide, the better chance we have of bringing a wide range of people to Jesus. Those check off my two biggest boxes: helping people in hurting communities and sharing the good news of Jesus Christ."

"Always look at *your* money, Quentin," his father had said. "The more you spend on unneeded things, the less money you'll have."

Greater Temple had bought the foreclosed property after the founder and pastor of the previous church died. He hadn't had any family or anyone to take over the church. Once Quentin had made the purchase, it only took about a year for the attendance to skyrocket. The church was more diverse and attracted many people who were not regular church attendees. In fact, many had never been a part of a church. The diversity had made Quentin's father a little uncomfortable, but the church services had never lost their Pentecostal flavor, and ministry in the community had accelerated.

Paying the bank and the CCBS had never been a problem… until COVID-19 wreaked havoc in the church and community.

Johnson lived in a multimillion-dollar home just outside the city near one of the state's premiere golf courses. After Quentin drove through a lavish motorized cast iron gate engraved with AJ, it took two additional minutes to reach the breathtaking stone home that looked more like a castle than a country estate. A masked butler opened the large front door to reveal cherry-wood imperial staircases that caused Quentin to wonder if the queen would soon descend. The marble floors were accented with a large oriental rug that looked like it should be locked in a vault. A three-story vaulted ceiling highlighted the rotunda, which was illuminated by a gaudy crystal-and-gold chandelier that looked like it had been snatched from a European museum. It was quite an entrance.

"Good evening. My name is Giles," the butler said. "Mr. Alonzo will be with you in a few minutes. He has instructed me to prepare you a drink and make you as comfortable as possible."

Quentin looked at the butler, who was dressed in a black suit with a white shirt and black bow tie. "Is your name really Giles?"

The butler rolled his eyes. "My name is Winston. But Mr. Alonzo pays me well to be Giles. So I am Giles inside these walls."

Giles led Quentin past a large living room area with lavish navy-blue Victorian furnishings trimmed in gold. Expensive artwork in large garish frames highlighted every wall. Quentin was taken to a waiting area with a large bar. Giles poured him a glass of imported white wine with a name Quentin had never seen. He waited more than fifteen minutes, enough time to admire the lush furnishings, stone statues, and elaborate geometric wall designs. The home's décor was mesmerizing.

Quentin was surprised when Johnson finally strolled into the room. He needed platform shoes to reach five feet tall. He was in his early sixties, but there was no gray to be found in his shoulder-length Jheri curl or his well-trimmed beard. He wore a tailor-made navy-blue suit with a white silk shirt and an iridescent blue, pink, and gray ascot that matched his mask. His blue Ferragamo loafers were worth more than Quentin's car.

When Johnson smiled, a gold tooth sparkled among his bleached white teeth. His glasses were large, custom-made, and gaudy and could have been confused for Aquamarine goggles. He looked like a cross between a pimp and a small-time entertainer.

"Rev, Rev," Johnson said, extending his fist. Each of his fingers sported a large gold ring. "Welcome to my humble abode. Would you like to freshen that drink?" He tilted his head, signaling for Giles to leave the room as he slipped behind the hand-crafted mahogany bar.

"No, this is good right now," Quentin said, trying to find a rhythm of talking and drinking while maneuvering his mask. "I love your home."

"Thank you. We put a lot of work into this. My wife loves going to Italy and Africa and bring back all these custom pieces. I told her that pretty soon we are going to run out of room."

They both laughed.

"Is it just you and your wife living here?" Quentin asked.

"No, sir. My mother-in-law lives in the west suite, but it's so far away I rarely see her," Johnson said. "My nephew lives in the pool house and works for me. But my wife and I don't have any children, though I have seven."

"Wow, you have seven kids? How old are they?"

"They range from thirty-seven to nine. Four girls and three boys."

Quentin had tons of questions but did not want to pry. "That means that you are probably a grandfather."

Johnson smiled, sending a gold glint flashed in Quentin's eye. "Yeah, I have three grandchildren. God is good."

"All the time."

"Rev," Johnson said as he mixed his drink. "I want you to know that I have admired your ministry for the past few years. You do great work in the community, and you've really utilized the new campus. That's why I invested in the church; I could see from the beginning that you were a visionary."

"Invested? From the beginning?" Quentin was confused.

"Oh yeah. I followed Greater Faith when your father was the pastor. We know each other rather well, though he doesn't have the highest opinion of me. When I heard he had gotten sick and might have to give up the church, I was pleased you were there to take over. The place needed some new blood. How's that feisty mother of yours?"

"You know my mother?"

"I know your whole family, son. *And probably a few you don't know about.*" Johnson laughed softly. "I told you I grew up in the neighborhood." He took his drink and led Quentin into his enormous boardroom. The table was large enough to sit twenty people. "Please have a seat. You hungry?"

"I haven't eaten in a while," Quentin replied. "If you know my family and obviously you understand the history of the Greater Faith, why all the threats about not paying you during this pandemic? You see we are still trying to do good work."

"Oh, the money thing is straight-up business," Johnson said nonchalantly. "If you talk to your finance people, you'll see that CCBS gives money to your church every month. It's a nice tax deduction, you know. Plus, like I said, I admire the work you're doing. I've been to your church several times. You bring a strong word, and the people love you. That's my religious life. Like most Black folks my age, I grew up in the church. But what *we* have to discuss is *business*. And I'm a different man when it comes to my money."

"The bottom line is we are having difficulty paying you and everybody else because of this virus," Quentin explained. "People aren't giving like they used to. Our offerings are down 30 percent."

"Are you paying Melton's Bank? They own the first, right?"

"Melton's Bank, like most lenders, gave us four months of deferred payments once we realized this pandemic was going to be with us a while. And we are working on refinancing the loan to give us lower payments."

"That's nice," Johnson said as he waved to his kitchen help, who brought in chicken kabobs and grilled shrimp. "But I can't do that. You really need to taste the kabobs. The recipe comes from Persia."

Quentin reached for a kabob. "You *can't* do it, or you *won't?*"

"It's all semantics, Rev. Can't, won't—it doesn't matter 'cause it ain't happening." He took a bite of chicken and calmly sipped his drink.

"So you're not willing to give us *any* concessions?" Quentin asked while chewing on one of the best-tasting pieces of chicken he had ever eaten. "You know people are struggling with sickness, job loss, fear, depression, and frustration and you're not willing to work with us on a modified payment plan?"

"That sounds like the problems of a pastor, not a financier. I got bills too," Johnson said. "I bet the electric bill for this house is more than your electric bill at the church. Plus, if I caved into everyone singing the 'I ain't got no money blues,' *I* wouldn't have no money. And that ain't happening."

"It's not like we don't want to pay. We haven't missed a payment in three years. That should be worth something."

Johnson grabbed two jumbo shrimp and dropped them into his mouth. He chewed slowly, seeming to enjoy every bite. "That *should* be worth something?" he said. "But it ain't worth much to me. You were just doing what you said you would do. It was a part of the contract. So that only means that you met your obligation. You don't get no bonus points for that."

"Wow, man. That's cold."

Johnson looked Quentin in the eye. "I want to ask you something that I wondered about since the beginning of our agreement." He paused and sipped his drink. "Why did you do it? Why would you get in bed with a guy like me? You must have asked around and heard I'm one *ornery* SOB. And there's no way you told your daddy."

Quentin smiled. "It's called faith and obedience, Mr. Alonzo. I believe in my God. I know what the church is doing is what God wants us to do. And maybe, just maybe, God wanted us to meet. Maybe there is a miracle you need to see to believe."

Johnson chuckled. "It looks like you're the one whose gonna need a miracle 'cause if I don't get my money, I gotta start doing things worse than the ten plagues."

"You can threaten me all you want, Pharaoh, I mean Mr. Alonzo." They both smiled. "But I ain't scared of you. Look, you'll get your money. It may take a little longer than we agreed on, but you'll get paid. You have my word. But *I believe* that our relationship is about more than this money. I'm here to open your eyes and maybe change *the direction of your life*."

"I like my life," Johnson said. "Things are good. And I can't let the word get out on the street that I cut some slack for a smooth-talking preacher. That ain't happening."

"There has got to be a better way to run your business than always using fear. You might think about using kindness and compassion."

Johnson laughed. "See, that's why me and religion couldn't make it. I heard all about love and kindness in Sunday school. But I found that, in the end, all that does is make you weak. I believe *your* savior Jesus Christ was weak. How he gonna let them hang him on a tree? You can't make it in business being weak. They'll crush you out there. That's why I'm known as the ruthless Jack-You-Up Johnson, and that gets me respect."

"Obviously you didn't stay in Sunday school long enough to learn the difference between weakness and meekness," Quentin began with a slight smile. "Jesus Christ was not weak, far from it. He was meek. The difference is that someone who is meek has the power but decides not to use it. And Jesus died on the cross because that was what he came to do. To die for our sins. But know that he had the power to stop all the madness, but his love for us put him on the cross."

"What good is it to have power and not use it?" Johnson asked.

"That's it. You can do more good when you don't flaunt your power, especially at the expense of others." Quentin paused and stared at Johnson. "Power can be used for good. That's what we try to do at the Greater Faith, helping the poor, hungry, down-and-out folks who no one else, especially people with power and prestige, aren't willing to help."

"That's insane," Johnson said, rolling his eyes. "If you don't use your power, people will run over you, especially as a Black man in this ruthless business."

"So when you die, and let's say I get the *pleasure* of doing your eulogy, is the only thing you want said, 'He was a mean, ruthless SOB?' Is that how you want to be remembered? Wouldn't it be great if your legacy was about a man who changed into someone who actually cared for those around him?"

"So you wanna make me a new creature?" Johnson asked sarcastically.

"Nope. I think you got the message for the day. I just want you to think about alternative ways of doing business and living your life. It's never too late to change. I wasn't always a preacher, you know. There was a time when we would have had to shoot it out instead of talking it out. But Jesus changed me."

"Look, preacher man, I just want my money."

"That ain't happening," Quentin said with a smile.

"What you say?" asked Johnson, sitting up in his chair.

Quentin continued to smile. "Look, if you can find an ounce of compassion and give me the same deal as the bank, four-month deference, we'll be ready to roll as usual."

Johnson stood up and began walking around the room like he was looking for something. He walked into the bar area and then came back to the boardroom.

"I've enjoyed the conversation, Rev, but I couldn't find no compassion anywhere. So you pay me my money or things will get ugly. You understand?"

Quentin stood up, prepared to leave. "It's already ugly. And it's you, your attitude, your approach to life *and* business. And if the Bible teaches one thing, it is that things don't end well for people like you. You'll get your money when we have it. Do your worst. Maybe you heard this when you were paying attention in church, but I stand on the truth: The battle with you is not mine. Thanks for the hospitality."

Quentin walked out of the room, trying to make a dramatic exit. He immediately found himself lost.

"Giles, please help the Rev get out of my house," Johnson said sternly.

Only a few minutes after leaving Johnson's home, Reggie called Quentin three times. Quentin knew things could get serious with Johnson, but he had to stand his ground. He felt like Luke Skywalker in *Star Wars*. Despite Johnson's ugly attitude and desire to frighten and bully, Quentin saw good in him. He had to look deep through a lot of pain, suffering, perceived disrespect, and anger, but he believed there was something there.

On the fourth call, Quentin answered. "What do you want, Reggie?"

"I want to know what you told Mr. Alonzo," said Reggie, who was obviously in panic mode. "He called me enraged. He wants to kill somebody."

"What's up with him anyway?" Quentin asked. "Why is he so hard?"

"It was rough for him when he first started," Reggie explained. "I heard a lot of white business owners fought to keep him from getting any capital and opening any businesses. He's filed for bankruptcy three times, and because check-cashing joints don't have the best reputation, he was getting pushback from his own community. Now everything is about revenge. He don't like nobody. Plus, he got that Napoleon thing going too."

"I can't trip on him right now," Quentin said. "I told him we would send him his money when we get it."

"That ain't gonna work, Q. I told you the man is off his rocker."

"I'm gonna let God take care of him. I've got to focus on the church, ministry, and helping some of the people out here who are really suffering because of this virus. I just left the man's home, and a couple of missed payments will not put him in the poorhouse. He'll be all right."

"You just better watch your six, bro," Reggie said. "He might want to make an example out of you."

"And God might want to make an example out of him," Quentin countered. "I'll talk at you later."

CHAPTER 8

PANDEMIC PASTORING

The next day, Quentin received the church's financial report for the last three months. Despite not having live worship services and scrambling to put together ways people could continue to praise, worship, serve, and give, he was surprised that giving was beginning to increase. In addition, because of the large attendance during online services, people who were not members of the church or no longer regular attendees were giving too.

But people were still getting sick. Most of the choir members had recovered from the initial infection, though two remained in the hospital. It seemed like every day Quentin was getting another call concerning someone in his congregation or social circle who had been infected by the virus. The numbers in the county and state were skyrocketing.

Quentin had yet to hear from the board of bishops, so he continued as the pastor of Greater Faith, working to let his congregation know he was still in charge. He began making daily calls to church members. Most were surprised that the pastor called, but their stories touched his soul. So many people were scared, lonely, isolated, and confused. Many had lost family members and were heartbroken because they'd had no opportunity to say goodbye in person or to have a decent homegoing celebration. Others asked if something like this was biblical and why God punished everyone, including the saints.

Quentin did his best to calm their fears and turn them to faith. He frequently read Psalms 91, which assured those who loved the Lord that God was with them during a plague. He also reminded them what the Bible said in Matthew 5:45b: "for He makes His sun rise on the evil and on the good and sends rain on the just and on the unjust."

The sadness of his members weighed heavily on Quentin. He knew he had been called to serve in this season. He understood that God had been getting him ready for this for a long time, but frequently he, too, was lost. He believed by faith that God was in the middle of all this. He prayed more than ever and read God's word daily, searching for the answers to his congregation's inquiries and finding an assurance that as things worsened, God was still in control. And he was dealing with his own challenges.

Vanessa was not pleased that Quentin was constantly going in and out of the house. She wanted to make sure their daughters were safe. She only went out for emergencies. Since Quentin was always heading somewhere, she made him do most of the grocery shopping while she homeschooled the girls. During the seven months of quarantine activities, Vanessa and the girls had only left the house three times.

"Is this ever going to end?" Vanessa asked one evening.

"It will end in God's time," Quentin responded.

"OK, I know that's the canned answer you give people in the church, but this is me, and I'm serious," Vanessa said. "I have great trust in God, but this is taking me to the edge. People are dying. We can't interact. We can't go to church. It seems everyone we know is in quarantine. And I love my babies, but being locked in this house with them for the past six months is beginning to affect my mental stability."

Quentin looked at his wife and could see the frustration in her eyes. "We aren't in control, and I'm not going to worry about things

I *can't* control. I honestly believe this is in God's hands, and I know *we* are in God's hands. All we can do is the best we can and continue to represent Jesus every day. I tell you what, you pick a weekend, and you can get away. I'll take care of the girls."

Vanessa gave her husband a doubtful gaze. It was the look that told him she questioned his conviction. "You gonna watch the girls *all* weekend?" she asked.

"Yes, I will," he said adamantly. "I know you need a break. I'll tape a sermon early in the week, and you can just go. I'll plan a weekend of fun and fantasy with the girls."

"I'm gonna take you up on that," she said. "And you cannot play the duct tape game or the all-day hide-and-seek. I know how you play with the girls."

"Wow, I was gonna play hide-and-seek, but if you insist, I will scratch that off the list."

"And the duct tape?"

"Yeah, yeah, we're cool. No duct tape."

"Not any kind of tape or rope or Velcro, Quentin."

He rolled his eyes. "You ain't no fun."

It turned out that Bishop Jenkins did have the virus and was not doing well. Quentin's father had tested negative initially, but had to quarantine for fourteen days. Cornell had kept a small bell by his bedside and rang it constantly to get his wife's attention. It seemed he'd always been in need of something, and just as Essie completed one task, Cornell had found something else for her to do. When he was hot, he had wanted her to fan him. When he was cold, he had asked Essie to bring more blankets. She had tried her best to be faithful, but she had contemplated leaving to see what her husband would do.

There was continued pressure to reopen the church, but Quentin read the news and had phone conversations with pastors across the country. He adopted caution as his primary approach to reentry.

"Pastor Q, you know that we were never supposed to worship

God over the telephone," Deacon Justice said during their weekly call. "That just ain't natural. We're being robbed of the presence of the Holy Ghost because we can't come to church."

Quentin replied, "But, Deacon, don't we always say we serve an omnipresent God? That means God is with us everywhere all the time. Remember what David wrote in Psalms 139:7–10: 'Where shall I go from your Spirit? Or where shall I flee from your presence? If I ascend to heaven, you are there! If I make my bed in Sheol, you are there! If I take the wings of the morning and dwell in the uttermost parts of the sea, even there your hand shall lead me, and your right hand shall hold me.' Doesn't that indicate that God is everywhere?"

"But it didn't say anything about the telephone or the internet," Deacon Justice replied.

"But if God is *everywhere*, why are you saying that God can't hear our worship or be a part of our services over phone lines or the internet? It sounds to me like you are putting technological limitations on God."

"You just twisting it all up, Pastor. You know what I mean. Church was never intended to be held like this, and it ain't biblical."

"But you don't really know that, do you?" Quentin asked. "If God is in control, and God is the Alpha and Omega like we always say, then God knew that this season in our lives would come. And maybe, just maybe, God wanted to see who would be willing to go to extraordinary measures to give Him praise and worship His holy name, no matter where or how we worshipped."

"I don't know. It just don't seem right."

"This sounds personal. I know you don't like the way we're doing church now, but at least we are able to do church."

"This is not church," Deacon insisted.

"The Bible says where two or three are gathered, the Holy Spirit would be there. It does not put limitations on the location of those two or three people. Neither does it prescribe a particular way these two or three should communicate. We need to stop complaining about what we don't have and seek God's face with what we are given. And I think this is an excellent opportunity to reach people who would never come *into* the church. Now they don't have to."

"If they weren't willing to come into the church, they weren't trying to find Jesus."

"Now you're saying that the only place to find Jesus is in a church building. Did I get that right?" Quentin asked.

"Pastor, I think the devil's got you." Deacon Justice hung up the phone.

The pastor and ministerial staff were fielding similar calls daily as people struggled with what had become the dreaded new normal for the church. The pandemic had caused everything to change, and the world was changing too. Not only because of the pandemic but also because of the death of a Black man, George Floyd, who was murdered by a policeman in Minnesota who put his knee on Floyd's neck for almost nine minutes. It was videoed and shown around the world. Protests and riots took place all over the country. The Black Lives Matter movement, which had been ignored for years, took center stage in protests for equal rights and an end to police brutality.

Quentin wrestled with what was happening across the country. He favored the protests because he knew the dangers of being a Black man in America, but when protests turned to looting and violence, he could not condone it. In addition, as a minister, Quentin believed that all lives mattered to God. That was not a popular stance and one he did not articulate frequently, but in his heart, he wanted equality for everyone.

Quentin went to the church office to handle his calls and administrative activities. He was also able to rehearse the taping of his Sunday morning sermons. One Tuesday afternoon, he had an unexpected visit from Todd Blake, one of the church's members. Todd was active in the men's ministry and a trustee. He was also one of the growing number of white members in the church. At least nine white and four Asian families were members, along with a large contingent of African and Hispanic members. Quentin was ecstatic that Greater Faith had evolved into a church of many flavors.

After knocking on the pastor's door, Todd came in fully masked. "Pastor, I know I should have called, but I was driving by the church and saw your car. I wondered if you had a minute to talk with me." Todd was the father of three children, who were always present for Sunday school. His wife, Rebecca Anne, was one of the teachers at the church's childcare center.

"Come on in, Todd. Have a seat. You're always welcome. I hope all is well with Rebecca and the kids. Y'all staying away from the rona I hope."

"Oh, they're doing fine, Pastor. Rona free as far as I know. I want you to know we miss coming to church on Sundays. The online service is OK, but it lacks a little fire. And the way we sing and praise at home just doesn't seem to make it."

"We're all learning to make adjustments," Quentin said. "What's on your mind today?"

There was a moment of hesitation. Quentin was learning to read people wearing masks, which was not easy, but he sensed Todd was troubled.

"Pastor, I'm struggling with what is going on with the Black Lives Matter activities. Not that I don't support what is happening, but people, members of the church, are treating us differently since the George Floyd incident."

"Really. How so?"

"We don't see many people because we spend most of our time in the house during the pandemic, but when I go to the grocery store, I get looks I never got before. Even some of the brothers in the men's ministry and the basketball team are short with me. And when I join some of the small group discussions on Zoom, the conversation seems to change when I log in. I don't understand."

"This is a challenging time for everyone, Todd," Quentin said. "You are our brother in Christ, know that off the top. But there is a lot of tension out there between whites and Blacks. Maybe what you're getting is a little overflow."

Todd shakes his head. "Pastor, I would not have brought my family to this church if I didn't feel comfortable with African Americans. We're all in this together. I don't even see color."

Quentin put his hand over his mouth and sat quietly as he framed his response. "I've got to stop you right there, and I don't want you to take this wrong, but you *do* see color. How your mind processes color makes all the difference, but the color of our skin in this society is undeniable."

"But, Pastor, let me tell you, I don't have a racist bone in my body."

Quentin did not know where this conversation was going. "Where are you from, Todd?"

"Born and bred in Louisiana."

"And how did your parents feel about African Americans?"

Todd dropped his head. "They were from the Deep South, Pastor. You know how that is."

"Yeah, I know. Which is why, despite your denial and how you have tried to change your life, you have racist DNA flowing through your veins."

Todd shook his head. "No, Pastor. No way."

"It's not your fault. And I am not saying that you are an active racist. But the roots of your life were planted in white privilege and watered with racism. You can't help yourself."

"I've been fighting it my whole life, Pastor. I played ball with brothers since the fifth grade. I hung out with them, went to their houses, and even dated a few Black women back in the day. Pastor, I've eaten chitterlings *and* hog maws. Didn't really like either one. And I don't like greens either, but my point is that I hung out with a lot of Black people. My parents weren't pleased, but I just didn't buy into a lot of the stuff they were spewing."

"And where is Rebecca from?" Quentin asked.

"She grew up in New Jersey. Her parents were way more liberal than mine."

"Well, let me share a secret that may be a reason for the alienation you are feeling with some of the Black folks in the church and beyond. My parents are from the South too. I grew up in a household that detested white people. My grandparents were from Alabama and were both as prejudiced as they could be. And that's the case with most of the Black people in the congregation. Our history makes us very skeptical of white people. That's how I grew up. It took me a long time to be comfortable around Caucasians because of the stories I heard and the names they were called in my house. I was taught to *never* trust white people. Never."

"Wow, that's a trip," Todd said.

"We're all learning how to deal with each other and battle the hate within," Quentin said. "We have made great strides at Greater Faith. Back when my father was the pastor, there were no white people in the church. You, Charles, and the rest of our newer members have added diversity here, and I think that's great. But it is not easy for everyone."

"And I'll admit, Pastor, that some of the stories you tell during your sermons don't make any sense to me. I know it is a part of the Black experience, and I can look around and see that all the Black people understand, but there are some Sundays when you lose me, at least in the beginning."

"I'm so sorry," Quentin said with a smile. "I tend to preach from my experience, and I've been Black all my life. But I'll keep that in mind in the future. It will be interesting to see how we all get along after the virus, Black Lives Matter, and the election."

"The Bible tells us to love our neighbor. It doesn't specify color; it specifies love," Todd said.

"You're right. But what happens in Greater Faith is not necessarily what happens outside these walls. Maybe that's why God has us outside the walls right now. Maybe we must learn to love unconditionally when not in the church because that is where the people who need Jesus live."

"What can *I* do?" Todd asked. "I don't want to leave the church, but I don't want people not liking my family or me because we're white."

"Like you said, Todd, it is all about love. First Corinthians 13 tells us about a love that has no restrictions. My advice to you is to keep loving everybody. Those who mistreat you will have to learn more about love. And based on this conversation, I'll preach our responsibility to love differently. But we are all growing in this thing, and we need the help of the Holy Spirit to bring it all together. I appreciate you coming by and sharing."

"Thank you for hearing me out, Pastor. I pray that God will continue using you to help us love one another."

Quentin's phone rang. He looked at the caller ID. "Todd, I've got to take this, but I will be praying for you and your family, and please pray for Greater Faith and me."

"I lift you up every day, Pastor. Thanks, and be blessed."

The caller informed Quentin that another member had been admitted to the hospital. He looked at the list he had compiled. This made fourteen people in the hospital, twenty-five at home in quarantine, and another twenty recovering. *When is this going to end, Lord? When is it going to end?* he wondered.

Quentin decided to clean out his email account. He had four hundred unread emails in the past month. He clicked on a few randomly.

> Pastor, please pray for me. I have been homeschooling my three children for four months, and I pray I don't kill'em. These little rascals are really trying me. Please pray for our family.
>
> Pastor, I want to apologize for not being able to pay my tithes. I lost my job three months ago,

and I have been living on meager savings and unemployment. I want to pay my tithes and help support the church. I know it is a sin if I don't, but for the first time in decades, I just don't have the money. Please ask God to forgive me for my disobedience.

Pastor, I would like to report that since the pandemic, I have stopped smoking weed. I have decided for the first time in twenty years not to buy marijuana. This is truly a miracle. God is so good. I just wanted to give you a praise report. As you always say, when God closes one door, he will open another. But I'll be honest, I am sure glad the liquor stores ain't closed.

Pastor Q, during this pandemic, I have taken your suggestion that I should read the Bible more. I have a lot of time on my hands now that I am not working, and I was anxious to get into the Good Book. What I have discovered is that I need glasses. I can't read a thing. And the only Bibles I have, the print is so small that all the words just run together. I'm just glad the Lord knows my heart.

Pastor Quentin, I do not understand why we are not having church. God wants us in the church because this virus will not harm true Christians. And until we are back in the building, I will withhold my substantial tithes checks. You need to be obedient to God and open the doors of the church.

Pastor, you just keep on preaching on Sunday mornings. I don't know how you do it with no one to preach to, but you bring the Holy Spirit into my house every Sunday. Things are bad out here with the virus, but with your singing and preaching, I'm doing just fine. Even when you open the church, I'm not coming back. Too dangerous. But I'll continue to send in my offering and watch on Zoom. May God continue to bless you.

Quentin spent another hour reading emails that ranged from sad to joyous. Some writing him were confused and others had seen the light during the time of quarantine. His head hurt as he turned off his computer and prepared to go home. He fought the temptation to spend a little more time on his computer, but he knew his trolling often led to ungodly destinations.

The phone rang again, and he wasn't ready for any more bad news. Then he received a text from his mother: *911*. He closed his computer and quickly dialed his mother's number.

CHAPTER 9

KNOCK HIM OUT

Quentin knew that if his mother used the 911 code, something serious was happening. He could only imagine how long it had taken her to remember how to text.

"Mom, this is Quentin. Is something wrong with Pops?"

"I just called you. Why didn't you answer the phone?" she asked.

"Do you know how many calls I get in a day? After a while, I stop looking at the phone."

"That's your fault," she said. "I told you not to put your real phone number in the church bulletin *and* online. That don't make no sense. Everybody and their momma can call you."

"I did that to be transparent, Momma. I wanted people to be able to reach me."

"Well, maybe you should try being translucent and get an answering service or at least a number that goes to voicemail."

He knew he could not win this reoccurring argument. "Mom, what's the 911?"

"It's your father," she said. "He's as sick as a dog who ate Tide pods for breakfast. He's coughing and weak and talking out of his head. He can't smell nothing, his temperature is 101.8, he won't eat, and all he wants to do is drink Nyquil and sleep."

In the background, Quentin could hear his father yelling: "I am not talking out of my head, woman. You need to tell the truth and tell that dog to stop barking."

"We don't have a dog!" she screamed. "You're out of your mind!" She paused and began to whisper. "Quentin, he has all the signs of the rona, but he refuses to go to the hospital."

"What do you mean he won't go to the hospital?" Quentin asked.

"You know your father is as stubborn as a constipated mule."

"Put him on the phone."

She handed the phone to Cornell.

"Son, can't nobody make me go to no hospital!" his father screamed, coughing loudly. "I'm trusting in God."

Quentin was furious. "Well, here is what God told me. The same God *you* trust. If you don't take your stubborn tail to the hospital, I'm gonna come over there, shoot you, throw you in the trunk of my car, and drop you at Adventist's front door. Do you understand?"

There is a pause. "You can't be talking to me like that," Cornell replied softly, obviously hurt by Quentin's tone.

"Pops, you're going to the hospital. It's up to you whether they treat you for coronavirus or coronavirus *and* a gunshot wound. Are you hearing me?"

"Boy, *you* are out of your mind. Plus, the gym is closed."

Quentin could not believe what he was hearing. "I'll shoot you, old man. I won't kill you, but you gonna be limpin' for a while."

"Essie, take this phone. That boy done lost his mind," Cornell barked.

His mother got back on. "He needs to go to the hospital, Quentin. I'm worried about him."

"You remember what we talked about?"

She hesitated. "You mean the special?" she asked.

"Yes, Momma, the special tea. You need to get him to drink the tea, and I'll be there in about thirty minutes."

"I can't remember what goes in it."

"It's already premade in the cabinet, remember? I'm on my way."

"I got it, baby. Hurry up."

Quentin dashed out of the church and proceeded to his parents' house. He hoped his mother could find the premixed bag of tea he put together for occasions like this. He had talked with his herbalist, who told him to combine Nighty Night Extra Strength tea with valerian root, melatonin, and chamomile. He knew if his father drank it, he would be out like a light in fifteen minutes. He also called Barbara at the hospital to inform her that he would bring in the bishop within the hour.

When he got to the house, his mother sat calmly at the kitchen table, sipping tea.

"You didn't drink the same tea you gave him, did you?" Quentin asked.

"Look at me and let me know if I look like I've lost all my senses," she said slowly. "No. If I put all that stuff in my system, you'd have two old people out like a light." She looked into the den, where Quentin could hear his father snoring. "He's been out for about ten minutes. How you gonna get him to the car?"

Quentin looked around the house. "You still got that old wheelchair?"

"The one I used when I had hip surgery is in the garage," his mother replied.

Quentin got the wheelchair and put his sleeping father in it. Over the last few years, Cornell had lost weight, making Quentin's mission a little easier. His mother put on her coat and picked up her purse.

Quentin looked at her and shook his head. "Momma, you cannot come with me," he said firmly.

"That's my husband of forty-seven years," she said with attitude. "If he's going to the hospital, I'm going with him."

"But they won't let you in because of the virus."

"I'd like to see them stop me," she snapped.

"Momma, you are not going up to this hospital throwing

punches and threatening people. That will only make things worse for Pops."

She looked at him, rolled her eyes, and took a deep breath. "Well then, I guess I won't go. But you tell them they better treat him right or I'm gonna pay them a *special* visit."

"We're in good shape. Sister Barbara Courtney from the church is one of the head nurses, and she knows we're coming. She'll take care of Pops."

"You talkin' about Sister Barbara with them bad teeth?"

"Momma, that's why you're staying right here. You'll say anything. I'll call you and give you an update."

"I'll stay here, but you know that girl got bad teeth. That's unacceptable when you got insurance."

Quentin put a mask on his father's face, lifted him into the car, and strapped him into the passenger seat. Cornell continued to sleep, rarely opening his eyes. He was only two blocks from the house when his mother called. Quentin answered on his car's Bluetooth system.

"What's up, Momma?

She was crying. "You take care of him. I love that stubborn old goat. Take care of him."

"I'll take care of him, but you gotta stop putting that bourbon in your tea. I'll call you later."

Quentin had the CarPlay system read some of his text messages on the ride to the hospital. It was through a message from the episcopal office that he learned that Bishop Jenkins had the virus and was in the hospital on a ventilator.

"If you have had contact with the bishop, please get tested immediately." Quentin looked at his father, who was sound asleep. He knew this did not bode well for him or his mother.

Nurse Barbara was waiting at the emergency room door. When Quentin looked inside, the waiting room looked like a mass shooting had occurred. The chairs were filled with masked people coughing and hanging their heads. Others were pacing in the room with bandages on their heads and splints on their arms. Several people lay on the floor, curled up in fetal positions. A putrid odor raced out of the room as the door opened wider, causing Quentin to take a few steps back. The technicians put Bishop Dillard on a gurney and quickly rolled him into the hospital.

Barbara looked at Bishop Dillard and asked Quentin, "Is he on drugs?"

"No. We just gave him an herbal mixture to relax him."

She glared at Quentin. "I don't think I want to know what kind of mixture you gave him, but I'll call you when I hear something."

"Any way you can get me in there?" Quentin asked.

"Not right now. I've never seen this many people in the hospital. Most are here because they won't wear masks. We're overflowing with virus cases, and we're almost at capacity. When we get Bishop in a room, and I will expedite that, we'll make plans for a stealth visit. But whatever you do, please do not bring the First Lady in here. She's too loud to be sneakin' anywhere. Let me go."

Quentin's shoulders drooped as he looked longingly at the closing hospital door. He walked slowly to his car as the seriousness of the situation began pressing on his shoulders. During the drive home, Quentin called family members to let them know the situation. His mother called him five times, and each time he had to tell her that he had not heard anything.

He decided to stop by the shores of Lake Trammel. Once there, he rolled down the windows and took a few deep breaths. It had been so much. His nerves were frazzled, but the setting sun reflecting off the calm lake waters seemed to rock his soul into a comfort state. With all that was going on with the church, church members, and now his father, he didn't know if he could take it. He had always tried to handle the pastoral pressure, but he was reaching his breaking point. That was when a familiar scripture, 1 Corinthians 10:13, popped into his spirit: *"And God is faithful. He will not allow the temptation to be more than you can stand. When you are tempted, he will show you a way out so that you can endure."*

"God please show me the way," he whispered.

Quentin learned later that night that his father was resting comfortably. They were waiting for the results of the COVID test, but Nurse Barbara told him that his father exhibited all the symptoms. They had put him on a pain reliever, antibiotics, and mild sedative, but he was breathing without a ventilator. They would know more in the morning. He had to make one important call.

"Hey, Nessa."

"I was wondering when you would call me," she said. "You know I got all kinds of news about Dad and the virus, and someone said he had cancer and a sleeping disorder."

Quentin chuckled. "No, it's not all that. But I am afraid that he has the virus. I got a text that Bishop Jenkins has the virus and is on a ventilator, and Pops was hanging out with him. Here's the deal: do you want me to come home?"

"Of course, I do." she said.

"I'm just thinking about the safety of you and the girls. I've definitely been exposed, and I don't need y'all to be infected."

"Baby, I want you home," Vanessa said. "I'll set up the bedroom in the basement for tonight, and we'll figure this out. But you sure ain't staying at no hotel. Just come through the downstairs entrance. And wear a mask. I'll come down to see you."

Quentin tried to slip in the basement door without making much noise because he did not want his daughters to hear him. The lower floor in his house had been constructed as an in-law suite for the parents. It had a well-equipped bedroom, a full bathroom, a lounge area with a large TV, a kitchenette with a small stove, a refrigerator, a microwave, and an air fryer. Little did he know this would make an excellent quarantine area. He was happy that his primary office was just above the basement bedroom, which meant the WIFI signal was strong. He had recently added a door at the base of the stairs for additional privacy.

The thought of not being with his family for two weeks disturbed Quentin greatly. His wife and daughters were his joy in the middle of sadness, sorrow, death, and sickness. He called Vanessa to let her know that he was home but advised that she not come downstairs. He asked that she bring some clothes, his laptop, and charging cords to the stairs, letting her know this would be a long process.

Vanessa brought down the items he requested and talked to him through the door. "How did things get so bad?" Quentin asked. "It feels like this is some kind of punishment."

Vanessa sat on the stairs. "I know this preacher; he's kinda cute," she said. "He always tells his congregation that our lives are a part of God's plan, not ours. He also says that God's ways are not ours, so we can never know what God is doing, but if we have faith, we know that all things will work together for good and when we find ourselves in new and different situations, there is a lesson to be learned."

Quentin chuckled. "That preacher sounds like a genius, a brilliant man. But I wonder if he had ever gone through anything like this."

"I know he's been through a lot, and God has always brought him through," she replied. "Oh, and he always says nothing is impossible with God."

"Thank you, Nessa. I'm exhausted. I'll call you in the morning. Tell the girls that daddy will see them soon."

"You'll see them?"

"We'll work something out."

Despite having a luxury foam mattress, Quentin did not sleep well that night. So many thoughts and scenarios leaped in his mind every time he turned over, and he always slept like a rotisserie. He saw his father's face, he felt his mother's pain, and words from the many sad emails sailed through the stormy seas of his mind. He thought of all those sick with the virus in his church, community, and country. He thought of his church family and all the people who depended on his leadership. He got hot and started sweating and wondered if 'rona was making her assault. He thought of his two daughters and wife, who were so close yet far away. All he could do was whisper, *"Lord, I'm gonna really need your help."*

The following day, Quentin woke himself up coughing. A vice grip tightened around his head, and a cement mixer was alive and churning in his stomach. It was difficult to breathe, and his body ached like multiple NFL linebackers had simultaneously hit him. And he kept coughing. He sat up and was lightheaded. He stared at the digital thermometer but knew the song it would sing. He finally pointed it at his head and looked at a temperature that did not surprise him: 101.5. He felt both hot and cold and could not imagine himself getting out of bed. With the bit of strength he had, he prayed. "Almighty God, I need your healing power right now. You know all that is going on with me because you created me. I declare that this virus is not greater than my God." He started coughing again. "I bind Satan and declare my healing in the name of Jesus."

He managed to get to his water and downed a bottle all at once. His head felt like a high-flying air balloon. He sent Vanessa a text: *Not doing well.*

She responded: *Do you need to go to the hospital?*
Give me a few hours, and I'll let you know.

Quentin found several pain pills and swallowed them slowly. His throat was so sore it felt like he was swallowing hot coals. He laid his head on his pillow to keep the room from moving. He finally fell asleep.

The next few days were not good for Quentin. He felt a little better, but the body pain and fever stayed with him like a close friend. His cough was like an unwanted guest who would not leave. He tried to do work but didn't have the strength. He talked with Vanessa several times a day but convinced her that he did not need to go to the hospital. He wanted nothing to do with the madness he had seen when he dropped off his father. He called his ministerial team and told them about his situation. All he could do was pray and sleep. He felt terrible.

On the third day, Quentin found the strength to write out his last will and testament. He was sure he wasn't going to make it.

Maybe this was God's punishment for the sin that continued in his life. Maybe if he had gotten the help. Maybe if he had not allowed that easily entangled sin such easy access to his heart. He asked for forgiveness, but he had done that so many times he knew God was tired of hearing it.

He usually did his morning devotion, but his notebook and Bible were upstairs. He had several Bibles on his smartphone and wanted to read scripture before his morning prayer. He was surprised that the Spirit led him to Psalms 57, where David was in despair, hiding from King Saul, who was trying to kill him. The entire chapter helped to ease Quentin's spirit, but the opening verse set the stage.

Psalms 57:1

> Have mercy on me, O God, have mercy on me,
> for in you my soul takes refuge.
> I will take refuge in the shadow of your wings
> until the disaster has passed.

Quentin wondered when this disaster would pass. He sent a text to his prayer warriors to explain the situation. He knew that would unleash a bevy of prayers, texts, and emails. In these times, he knew most people would be praying for themselves, but he had been called to a greater responsibility, so he prayed for others.

He prayed for his father, who was still in the hospital, and for his mother, who he knew was at home worrying. He prayed for all those in his family and church family who were not only dealing with the devastating effects of the virus and the travails of life. He prayed for all the doctors, nurses, and caregivers who were stretched to the limit during this time. He prayed for the seniors in his church who had contracted the virus and were now alone in the hospital or convalescent home. He prayed for Bishop Jenkins, who was in a life-or-death struggle. He prayed until drops of sweat rolled off his forehead. After praying for others, he felt better.

He knew he should have turned off his phone before praying because it kept vibrating, and his text tones were popping off the phone.

"Lord, I can't take much more. I am only one man. Everyone calls me for prayer and encouragement, but that's what *I* need."

He remembered the last verse of Psalms 57 after David had written about his steadfast heart and a desire to continue to praise God despite the situation.

Psalms 57:11

Be exalted, O God, above the heavens;
let your glory be over all the earth.

After concluding the prayer and singing "Thank You Lord," as best he could, Quentin went to his phone. Of the eight calls he had received, five were from his mother. He knew she was worried, but he had to do anything to keep her from making a scene trying to get into the hospital. He checked his text messages, which included posts from Nurse Barbara, who said his father was doing well and responding to the medication. At least he had good news for his mother.

Essie picked up the phone quickly "Well, it's about time you called," she said. "I am your mother, and I take precedent over anyone you have on the phone. Do you understand?"

"You rank real high, Momma, but I was in my devotion talking to Jesus."

"Oh, Jesus," she said before hesitating. "All right then. But know that Jesus is the *only* one you can talk to instead of me. How's your father?"

"I heard from Nurse Barbara, and she said he was doing well."

"Did you talk to her or get a message?"

"I got a message."

"Why didn't you call her?"

"Because I got a message."

"Y'all young people and all this texting and twixting is ridiculous. You should have talked to her."

"She was going to tell me the same thing that was in her text."

"She might have been lying. You can't tell if someone is lying in a text. You need to see their face and hear their voice."

"Momma, why would she lie to me?"

There was a long pause. "I'm going to the hospital."

"Momma, I have told you that they will not let you in no matter how much screaming or quoting the Bible you do."

"I'm going up there and speak in tongues."

"Then they'll admit you as a lunatic or someone who had a stroke."

"At least I'll be inside."

"You'll be strapped to a gurney, filled with drugs, and taken to the nearest mental hospital."

"I wish they'd try," she said with attitude.

"Momma, let's call the doctor. Maybe that will put your mind at ease."

"You know that doctor's gonna lie."

"Not everyone lies, Momma. I'll call and put you on three-way."

"Three-way? That sounds like some kinda sex thing. Are *you* sick?"

Quentin dropped his head. He had become accustomed to this kind of behavior from his mother, who had been letting it all hang out the last few years. As the First Lady of the church, she had always been refined and reserved, but that woman retired when her husband retired.

"I am in quarantine," Quentin said.

"You got the rona too?"

"It's precautionary. I've been in close contact with Pops and Bishop Jenkins, so chances are great I'm infected. And to be truthful, I have been feeling terrible for the past few days."

"That means—" She begins to wail. "Oh Lord, that means I got the rona too. Not like this, Lord. Please not like this. Don't take me out like this."

"Momma, calm down, please. You need to take the test, but there is no guarantee that you've got it." He hears pans banging. "What you doin', Momma?"

"I'm trying to see if I can smell this food."

"Can you?"

"Greens smell like greens to me."

"Have you taken your temperature?"

"Hold on."

He heard her walking through the house and opening cabinets. Then he heard a beep.

"It says I'm 96.9. Oh Lord, that's too low. I got the reverse rona."

"Momma, you're fine."

"My temperature is supposed to be 98.6. I'm dying in reverse."

"Momma, stop it. 96.9 is fine. You'll live, and you're probably rona free. And by the way, dying in reverse is living, you know."

"You ain't no doctor," she snapped. "What you know about it?"

"I know Momma, I know. Let me try to get the doctor, and I'll call you back."

"Yeah, I need to talk to a real doctor. I'm freezing cold and burning up at the same time."

CHAPTER 10

HEALING PRAYERS

Quentin was still not at full strength by the end of the quarantine, but he was getting stronger every day. He decided it was time to turn off his phone. It seemed that every two minutes, someone was calling or texting him. He just wanted to get away from it all. As he pulled out his phone to turn it off, he saw that he had received four calls from Nurse Barbara, and she never called him. He called her with fear standing at the door of his heart.

"Sister Barbara, what's going on? I see you've been trying to reach me."

"It's your father. He's been asking for you. He won't let anyone touch him or give him any medicine until he sees you."

"I thought you told me he was doing better."

"He was, but something snapped. You need to get down here if *you* are feeling better."

"I'm still a little achy, but at least I can breathe. Those were the roughest fourteen days of my life."

"We live with that pain from hundreds of patients every day," Barbara said sadly. "But it keeps me prayed up. You need to get here quickly. I'll keep praying for you and your father."

"How can I get in? Do you want me to do the side door thing again?"

"Not this time," she said. "Tell them at the front desk to ask for me and that you are there to get your coronavirus test, and I'll take it from there."

These trips to the hospital were getting old for Quentin. His imagination ran like Usain Bolt as he sped through the city's streets. He wondered if his father was dying. He thought about his mother. He had neglected to turn off his phone, and the calls and messages kept flowing in.

He turned on the radio and tried listening to smooth jazz to calm his mind, but nothing worked. He thought about listening to country music but quickly changed his mind. His head was throbbing, and his stomach growled, reminding him that he had not eaten. He was lightheaded, which always happened when he didn't drink enough fluids. He knew he was a mess, but he had to see about his father.

After talking to one of the police officers at the door who knew he was the pastor of Greater Faith, Quentin walked slowly into the emergency room. With his mask on and the bill of his cap pulled over his eyes, he could not believe the sight. Patients filled every stall and hallway. Doctors and nurses looked like they were participating in a human demolition derby as they raced from patient to patient. He knew things were bad, but this was absolute madness.

"You can't be in here, sir," one of the nurses said.

"I'm looking for Sister, I mean, Nurse Barbara Courtney. I'm here for my COVID-19 test."

"There are plenty of places outside this emergency room to be tested. You'll have to leave."

"I've got him, Cynthia. I've got him," said Barbara, who appeared out of nowhere.

The nurse stared at Barbara. "He shouldn't be in here to take a test. But that's on you."

Barbara rolled her eyes. "Come with me," she said to Quentin. She moved quickly through the crowded hallway to the stairs. They went up two flights and through a door. She took him to a room where his father lay in the bed, eyes wide open.

"Is that you, Little Q?" Cornell asked with a hoarse voice. His father had not called him Little Q in decades.

"Yeah, Pops, it's me," Quentin said, breathing heavily. "How you doing?"

His father was gasping for air and trying to talk. He touched his lips, and Barbara brought him a glass of water and a straw. He sipped hard and took several deep breaths. "I'm glad you're here, son. We gotta talk." His voice was a bit stronger, but he appeared weak.

"I'll leave you two alone," Barbara said. "Bishop, if you need something, push your button."

He nodded to her.

"Son, I might not make it from this," his father said softly. "It feels like a 350-pound lineman is sitting on my chest. And it don't feel good." He tried to laugh but started coughing.

"Pops, maybe you shouldn't be talking. Trust me, I know. It had me down for almost two weeks."

"No. I gotta say this before I meet my maker. It's the only way I'll get a better seat."

Quentin knew things were bad. The seat reference was one of his father's favorite sayings. He always told Quentin that how you acted and treated people while alive determined where your seat would be in heaven. He said that people who gave their lives to Christ but lived like sinners might make it to heaven, but they would be seated in the back rows. It was always his father's goal to be up front to get a good look at Jesus.

"What do you have to tell me, Pops?"

Cornell touched his lips again, and Quentin gave him some water. Cornell pressed a button so the bed would sit up. He signaled for Quentin to come closer. "I wanted to apologize to you, son. I have not been right by you."

"No, Pops. You've been a great father."

"Hush up, boy. This is my confession," his voice was getting stronger. "Ever since you took over the church, I've been fighting you behind the scenes."

It took a moment for the words to settle in Quentin's mind. "What?"

"I'm the root of most of your opposition," Cornell said with closed eyes. "I had my people on the boards and ministries, and I was trying to make you look bad, trying to get them to remove you as pastor."

That news fell on Quentin like an anvil. "But why, Pops? I thought you wanted the church to stay in the family."

"No. I wanted the church to stay with *me*. It was *my* church," he said firmly before coughing loudly. He was breathing deeply and sweating. "It was all I knew how to do, and once you took it, I felt like a nobody."

"I didn't *take* the church, Pops. You had a stroke, remember? You were sick, and we didn't know if you'd get well enough to return. I didn't even want to be the pastor. I never thought that was my calling. The jurisdiction gave me the church with your blessing, I thought."

"I just did that because I thought it would be easier to get it back if you had it."

"But why, Pops? Why did you come after me?" There was a long silence. "You all right, Pops?"

"The Bible tells us that pride comes before the fall," his father said, speaking slowly but deliberately. "I had too much pride and a hunger for position, power, and prestige." He began breathing deeply again. Quentin could see his heart rate rising on the vital sign monitor; his blood pressure was starting to spike too.

Quentin's mind tried to tell him that maybe his father was delirious. But a quick mental tour of his repeated struggles in the church revealed that certain people had tried to stop him at every turn. He had never imagined the opposition had come from his father.

"And the worst part is," his father began before touching his lips again. "I am why you couldn't get the extra money you needed to buy the new church. I sabotaged your application. I was a fool."

Quentin was speechless. He just stood there with his eyes closed, not knowing if he should lash out or leave.

"I need you to forgive me, son. I need you to understand that what I did was out of pride and jealousy because you were doing so well, and no one needed me anymore. The Bible says you should forgive me, and I pray you will."

Suddenly, anger sprang up in Quentin like a wildfire buoyed by hurricane-force winds. Everything he had gone through had been his father's making. And Cornell had done it while smiling to his face and pretending to give good counsel. Quentin then knew that Bishop Jenkin's ploy to take over the church was orchestrated by his father, who wanted his power back.

"I don't know if I can forgive you, Pops," Quentin said while still searching for the reality of the situation. "What you did was unacceptable and disgusting for someone who calls himself a child of God, much less a pastor *and* my father. You're despicable."

Tears dripped from Cornell's closed eyes. "I know. You're right. That's why I'm suffering now. But I didn't want to leave here without setting things right with you."

"Pops, I got Mr. Alonzo threatening to do violence to me and my family because the church can't pay him back. And that's on you. I'm out here living in fear, wondering what I'm going to do, and you did all this for a little power?"

"Alonzo? Oh no. You didn't get the money from Alonzo, did you? I heard the rumors but didn't want to believe them. That man is a snake, a subterranean venom-filled snake."

"It looks to me like birds of a feather flock together," Quentin replied.

There was a long pause. "I deserve that," Cornell said softly. "But I'm trying to make things right."

"That's gonna take a lot of work, Pops. I still love you and want you to get better, but you hurt me bad."

"Son, you're the right man for the job," Cornell said, coughing slightly. "Despite my jealousy, you've done so much to grow the church's ministries. You're helping people. And your decision to close the church was the right one. This virus is a stone-cold killer. You are the man God positioned to lead the church in this season. Not me. I see everything clearly now. They say that happens before you die."

Quentin was doing his best to fight back anger and pain when he heard from the Lord. "Pops, this ain't your day to die. I forgive you only because God has forgiven me for so much. But when you get well, you and me gonna talk. Let me pray for you."

On his keychain, Quentin had a small container with sanctified oil. He opened it, poured half of it onto his father's forehead, and laid his hand on the oil. He felt what seemed to be an electric surge flow throw his hand. His father's eyes popped open as tears flowed. Quentin cried too as he began to pray.

"Heavenly Father, the Lord God our healer," Quentin began. "There are multiple wounds I am asking you to heal today. First, my father is sick with this virus, but the virus is not greater than you. I know that for a fact. Heal him in the name of Jesus. Next, Lord, heal my pain from what I have heard today. I am trying to process it and can't understand it, but you said that all things work together for those who love the Lord and are called according to His purpose. So even this, Lord, is working for my good. And Lord, please forgive my father. Your word says that if we confess our sins, you will forgive us and purify us from all unrighteousness. So God, in the powerful name of he who cannot fail, in the name of Jesus, I lift up this prayer and thank you for healing and forgiveness on this day. Amen."

Barbara burst into the room. "Oh, it's hot in here," she said, fanning her face with her hand. "Pastor, you've gotta leave. The doctors will be here in a few minutes." She looked at the monitor. "Oh my. His fever has broken." She looked perplexed. "And his respiration numbers haven't been this low since he got here." She looked at the pastor with wide-eyed amazement.

Quentin smiled. "The fervent prayer of a righteous man makes tremendous power available, dynamic in its working. James 5:16 is right on point."

"Well, let's get you outta here. Bishop, I'll be back to see you."

As Quentin turned to leave, his father grabbed his arm. "Thank you, son. May God continue blessing you."

"I'll see you in a few days, Pops. Be blessed."

Barbara hurried down the hallway, hoping none of the doctors would notice Quentin. As they turned the corner, a patient was being pushed down the aisle in a wheelchair. His head was hanging, his mask covered only his mouth, and he seemed to moan in pain. He was dressed in an expensive brown leisure suit with handmade Berluti Scritto loafers. As he lifted his head slightly and caught Quentin's eye, the pastor stopped suddenly. As the patient was wheeled into a nearby stall, Quentin recognized the unmistakable well-kept Jheri curl.

"Hold on, Sister Barbara," Quentin called out as the nurse who had wheeled the man into the waiting room left.

"Pastor, we've got to go," Barbara said adamantly.

"Hold on, hold on," he said, walking quickly to the waiting room, where his suspicions were confirmed. It was Alonzo Johnson, coughing heavily and breathing unevenly. He looked up and saw Quentin.

"What you doing here, Rev?" he whispered, coughing softly.

"What are *you* doing in here? You ain't looking too good," Quentin said.

"I got this virus," he said, coughing and holding his chest. "I got it bad, man."

Quentin quickly pulled out his small container and poured oil into his hand. He placed his hand on Johnson's forehead and felt a jolt of divine energy.

"In the name of Jesus," Quentin began. He prayed for immediate healing and the ability for Johnson to breathe. When Quentin opened his eyes, he saw Johnson holding up his hands and whispering, "Thank you, Jesus."

Water pooled in Johnson's eyes as he repeated, "Thank you, Jesus, oh thank you, Jesus."

"Lord, this is your son, and you told us that we could ask for anything," Quentin continued. "And today, I ask for your healing power to flood this room and overwhelm your son. Shock the doctors and nurses, Lord, and prove to Alonzo Johnson right here and right now that you are a miracle-working God."

The curtain opened. "Pastor, we gotta go," Barbara said, as she looked at Quentin. "Why is every room you are in so hot?"

Quentin smiled. "We declare your healing in this place right now. Amen."

"Amen," Johnson said firmly.

"Gotta go, Mr. Johnson. I'll call you."

He was able to slip away from the rooms without being detected. Barbara took him down to get his COVID-19 test before leaving the hospital. Afterward, he sat in his car, exhausted. He could not believe what his father had told him, and he could not believe that he had run into Alonzo Johnson. The prayers had utterly drained him. He fell asleep in his car and woke to Vanessa's unique ring tone on his phone.

"Where are you?" she asked.

It took Quentin a couple of seconds to find his bearings. "I must have fallen asleep in the car."

"Quentin Elisha Dillard," Vanessa responded in an elevated tone, letting Quentin know she was not pleased. "I have told you about driving when you're that tired. And you're not entirely well yet."

"I'm not driving, baby. I'm not driving. I'm in the parking lot at the hospital. I saw Pops—that was wild—and prayed for him. Things are wild in that place. We need to pray for everybody in there. I took my COVID test and should hear something in a few days."

"You rest before you get on the road. Let me know when you get home. I will leave some food for you downstairs. Are you sure you're all right?"

"I am exhausted, confused, and spiritually wiped out. But other than that, I'm doing great."

"That's just another day for you."

They both laughed.

"I'll call you when I get home."

CHAPTER 11

STONE COLD KILLER

Quentin turned off his phone and slept like a baby when he finally arrived home. He nibbled on the food Vanessa had left for him, but he did not have a big appetite. When he finally woke up, he was shocked that it was 11:00 a.m. He had a slight headache and a noticeable rattling in his chest, but he felt better than he had just a few days earlier. When he turned on his phone, messages poured in like a waterfall.

Vanessa came into the room for her daily husband inspection. "Are you sure you're feeling better?" she asked through her mask.

"I feel like I just rolled off my deathbed, "Quentin replied. "There are some residual effects, but I am almost a new creature. Any word on Pops?"

"The good news is your father is doing better and will probably be released in a day or two. But he can't go home if your mother's sick."

"Let's pray Momma doesn't have the virus," Quentin said. "Oh, Lord, you *know* I am praying for that."

"How can she not have the virus?" Vanessa asked. "She has been around you, your father, *and* Bishop Jenkins, who seems to be getting better, by the way."

"I'm gonna put Momma in God's hands and declare all things

are possible," Quentin said, coughing slightly. "And I pray you and the girls are clear too."

Amazingly, it turned out that neither his mother nor Quentin's immediate family tested positive. He got an earful from his mother.

"You just ain't tough enough," Essie said during one of her daily calls. "I wasn't gonna let no rona mess with me. You men are just as soft as pillows."

"I'm glad you aren't infected, Momma," Quentin countered, " 'cause you would have been difficult to deal with. God knows who can handle this thing. How's Pops doing?"

"You should be askin' how am *I* doing trying to take care of your very needy father. He's as feisty as a hungry bear waiting in line at the Golden Corral," his mother said. "They had to put him in your old bedroom so I wouldn't get sick, and he's 'bout to lose his mind."

"You take care of him and tell him I'll come to see him in a couple of days."

A few days later, Quentin went to visit his father.

Cornell was in great spirits when Quentin entered his old bedroom. His voice was strong and his laughter even stronger. He seemed to be glowing as he welcomed his son with a gigantic hug.

"We can hug because we both survived the rona. Ain't God good," his father said.

Earlier in the day, Cornell had seen his grandchildren and had a wonderful time.

"It's good to see you, son," Cornell said. "Aren't we glad God is still in the healing business?"

"You look great, Pops. Are you sure you didn't sneak some of that good medicine out of the hospital?"

"When I got outta that place, I didn't want to take nothing, including the memories. I do remember you stopping by and praying for me. There was power in that prayer. But how did you get into the hospital?"

"I still have a few connections. I'm just glad you got out and are doing well."

"I haven't felt this good in a while," his father said.

Essie brought her son a tall glass of iced tea and her husband an ice water.

"Why don't I get tea?" Cornell asked.

"Because you have diabetes and just got out of the hospital with the virus. You better be glad you can swallow," Essie quickly replied.

"How you doin', Momma?" Quentin asked. "I'm still trying to figure out how you didn't get the rona."

"God knew somebody had to take care of your father, and I drew the short straw."

"Essie, leave us be," Cornell said, using his hand to shoo her out of the room. "I need to talk with my son. And thank you for the water."

She gave her husband a strange look because it was rare that he thanked her for such a simple task. But since returning from the hospital, he had been thanking her constantly. She guessed his experience had humbled him.

Once she left the room, Cornell sat up and turned off the TV. "Son, I know we had a conversation in the hospital."

"Are you going to tell me that you were out of your head on drugs and nothing you said was true?" Quentin asked.

Cornell smiled. "That is an option, but that wouldn't be correct. I remember very clearly what I told you." He hesitated. "And unfortunately, it was all true. I just wanted to apologize again because my actions were not Christlike. God and I had several intense conversations while I was in the hospital. I often wonder why God speaks so clearly when we're sick, but I now realize that might be the only time we're willing to be still and listen."

"So, what deep revelation did God give you?" Quentin asked.

His father smiled, looking into space like he was reliving the moments. "Where shall I begin... I need you to go to that drawer over there." He pointed to a small table with a single drawer in the corner of the room. "Bring me that big envelope."

Quentin did as he was asked. Cornell reached into the envelope and pulled out a stack of personal checks. "I need you to take these to the church." He handed the stack of checks held together by a large rubber band.

"What are these?" Quentin asked.

"They're my tithes checks," Cornell replied, dropping his head.

Quentin flipped through the stack. Some of the checks were three years old. Quentin was confused. "What are all these checks doing here?"

Cornell took a deep breath and wiped his hand over his face. "For a long time, my pride was guiding my actions," he said. "I wrote those checks because I have always been a tithe payer, but I wasn't going to give them to the church … until *you* were gone."

Quentin glared at his father. "What?"

"As insane as that sounds now, that is how right it felt every month when I wrote the check and put it in the drawer."

"Why would you do something like that, Pops? That's insane."

"I wanted my church back," he said softly. "You were in the way. I didn't think you would be able to handle all the responsibilities. When you're a pastor, preaching is the easy part. I knew you could preach, but handling administration and dealing with the staff and congregation is what makes most pastors want to throw in the towel. Once you failed, they would ask me to come back and save the day. But you proved me wrong. You did an excellent job. I guess you had a good teacher." He chuckled softly.

Quentin's mind was swimming in a festering pool of disbelief. "Pops, I'm still having a tough time digesting all this. If you wanted the church so bad, why didn't you just say something? I wasn't all that excited to take it over. That was *never* my plan. And when I came to you for advice, you always helped me. This doesn't make sense."

"I was fighting a vicious internal battle," Cornell said. "It's probably what made me sick. I wanted the church but didn't want to see you fail. Well, I did want you to fail, but I don't know. It was like Paul wrote in Romans, chapter seven, I think." He reached for the old Bible that was always near him. He quickly thumbed through the pages. "Here it is." He read the passage aloud.

Roman 7:15–20

> I do not understand what I do. For what I want to do I do not do, but what I hate I do. And if I do what I do not want to do, I agree that the law is good. As it is, it is no longer I myself who do it, but it is sin living in me. I know that nothing good lives in me, that is, in my sinful nature. For I have the desire to do what is good, but I cannot carry it out. For what I do is not the good I want to do; no, the evil I do not want to do — this I keep on doing. Now if I do what I do not want to do, it is no longer I who do it, but it is sin living in me that does it.

"I would say that I don't know what got into me, but I know it was Satan," Cornell admitted. "He had me so wrapped up, I couldn't think straight. I made a lot of bad decisions. I'm so sorry."

Quentin was glad his heart rate was not connected to a monitor. He suddenly had a headache that pounded his temples like a bass drum.

"Pops, I don't even know what to say."

"Just say that you forgive me, son. I know I have done some terrible things. I have been asking God for forgiveness for weeks. Now I need to know you can forgive me so we can move on."

"It's not that easy, Pops," Quentin said. "And does Momma know about these uncashed checks?"

"She most certainly does not. That's why I hid the checks in your room," Cornell said. "If she knew I was holding back tithes and the reason why, she might leave me. After she shot me. And I can't have that. I love that old girl. I'm hoping you won't tell her."

"Pops, I don't know what I'm going to do," Quentin admitted, still confused. "This continues to get crazier by the day. Look, I forgave you at the hospital, so we're good. I still don't understand the driving force behind what you did, but I'm glad it is out in the open. But moving forward on is going to be tough. I can't trust you anymore. Is there anything else you need to tell me?"

"Look, if I happen to leave here, and I ain't planning an early departure, you may hear some unpleasant things about me. There may be some accusations. I want you to know I am innocent."

"Exactly what are they going to say you did?"

"The exact details are not important. Just know that no matter what, I did not do it. I can't say I have been pure in this assignment, but sometimes strange things happen."

Quentin did not know what to expect. He could sense that his father was off his game in a good way. He was more talkative and cheerful, though a bit more morbid than usual.

"I just want you to keep on preaching God's word and leading the people as God leads you," Cornell said. "I know you will be a great pastor, and Greater Faith will continue to grow when all this corona mess is over. Maybe not in the way you envision but be open to growth in various ways. And I'm certain the financial challenges you face will be reconciled and the church will overflow with resources and ministries."

"You going all prophetic on me?"

"Hear me, son. Take care of all your people. It will serve you well. You were called to lead this church when you were just a child. I couldn't accept it then, and maybe that's when my heart started to harden, but it has come to fruition, and I am finally at peace."

"I was called to lead Greater Faith as a child? What are you talking about?"

His father closed his eyes. "Sister Henderson knew all the time."

"Sister Henderson. Are you talkin' about Carretha's mother?"

"Yeah, the prophetic gift has run in that family for a long time," Cornell said. "During one tarry service, Sister Henderson told me that my son would be the pastor and lead a great expansion of the church. You were just a kid, running around the church, getting into all kinds of trouble. I didn't see it. I brushed it off as the mindless ramblings of a want-to-be prophet, but she most definitely had the gift."

"You never told me before."

"I didn't see the need. When I got too sick to pastor and they gave the position to you, Sister Henderson's words came back to me like a high-speed boomerang, rest her soul. I learned a valuable lesson about God sending people to us with a word to help us along the way."

"Is that what you're doing for me? Giving me a word?" Quentin asked.

"Maybe I am," Cornell said. "I know you need to be there for your family and love your wife because when everyone turns against you, Vanessa will be by your side. And as I have always told you, be bold, courageous, and not afraid because God is with you." Cornell took a long sip of his water and breathed deeply. "You just don't know how good it feels to be able to breathe again," he said.

All that his father had told him felt good but strange. He talked with his mother for a while, not divulging the secret, and went home to spend more time with his family.

Later that night he got a call from his mother. She appeared to be crying. "Quentin, he's gone," she said quietly.

"What are you talking about, Momma?"

"Your father, he's gone."

"Where's Pops now?" Quentin asked.

"He's sitting in his chair," she said matter-of-factly.

"Did you call the funeral home?"

"No, I called you," his mother said. "You're the son, the pastor, and now the head of this household. I need you to take care of the details. You know I'm not good at that stuff."

Quentin knew he would have to take care of *all* the arrangements. Mentally, he was not ready to funeralize his father. And in the COVID-19 environment, funerals were very different. "OK, Momma. I'll call Justin's Funeral Home, and I'm heading over there."

Vanessa was shocked when Quentin shared the news.

"But he was so energized today. He talked to the girls and even played with them. And he had a few encouraging words for me, and he looked so... Oh my God, that was the glow, wasn't it?"

"Yeah, I saw it. Momma saw it too. But we were just hoping he was healed. It turns out he was on the runway headed home. He's with the Lord now."

News of Bishop Dillard's death spread like a California wildfire. Quentin's cell and house phones rang constantly. His voicemail filled up in a matter of hours. When he arrived at his parents' home, his father looked like he was in a peaceful sleep. Quentin took the remote out of his hand and waited for the funeral home representatives. He did not know how his mother was going to handle the death of her husband.

"This is about the third time I thought he was gonna die," she said, sitting at the kitchen table with a dazed look in her eyes. "After his first stroke, it took months for him to recover. Remember that? I didn't think he would ever talk again. And the second stroke was worse. And once they took the church, I think he *wanted* to die. He took that hard. Then this rona mess came, and I couldn't go see him in the hospital. I was just waiting for the call. But he knew his days were numbered. He told me so."

"He told you?" Quentin asked.

"Yeah, he said he had some kinda vision in the hospital that he was in heaven. I thought he was talking out of his head. I guess he wasn't."

The phone at his parents' house was continuously ringing.

Quentin tried to convince his mother that she did not have to answer every call, but she felt it was her duty to talk to everyone. He thought it took her mind off the situation. They had the choice to have the funeral at the funeral home or the church. Quentin knew his father would not appreciate a funeral home funeral, so he decided to hold the services at the original downtown church site with COVID-19 restrictions for the going home celebration.

"Momma, I will do the best I can to plan this homegoing."

"You don't have to," she said.

"What do you mean?" he asked.

She stood up and began walking to the rear of the house.

"Where are you going?" Quentin asked.

"Just hold your horses," she replied as she walked toward Quentin's bedroom. She came back holding a manila folder and handed it to Quentin. "You don't have to plan it because your father already did. Every aspect of the program has been covered. He has you doing the eulogy."

"What?" Quentin said in shock. "I thought one of the other bishops would do that."

"He wants us to follow his instructions explicitly, which means you *will* officiate and do the eulogy."

"He can't do anything if I don't."

She gave him a familiar gaze. "You will do as your father requested. End of story." Her expression turned inquisitive. "Your father didn't happen to give you a stack of checks, did he?"

Quentin started to laugh. "You knew about that?"

"I made it my business to know about almost everything. I didn't say anything to him, just let him be as stubborn and hardheaded as he wanted to be. God, I loved that man. But sometimes…"

Essie was extremely emotional when the representatives of Justin's Funeral Home came to pick up Cornell's body. Miles Justin, the owner, came for this pickup.

"Mrs. Dillard, I want you to know we will take excellent care of the bishop. We did a lot of work together, probably more than one hundred funerals. I never thought I would be burying him. He was a great man."

"Yes, he was," Essie said, wiping her eyes and leaning on Quentin.

"Any idea when you want to have the funeral?"

"We'll have to give you a call," Quentin said. "There will be a lot of church officials coming in from out of town. We need to give them time to make arrangements. We'll let you know in a few days."

As they rolled the body out of the house, Essie sobbed. "What am I gonna do now?" she asked.

"Momma, you're gonna do what you've always done. Survive with style. You know Pops wouldn't want it any other way."

For Quentin, it was like he was in a dream, a very bad dream.

The homegoing celebration was lively, which is what Cornell Dillard would have wanted. Attendance was limited because of the COVID-19 restrictions, but Greater Faith worked hard within the guidelines to have gospel music and reflections filled with laughter, truth, and an acknowledgement of the greatness of God.

All the denomination's bishops were in attendance except Bishop Jenkins. An announcement was made that he was making a miraculous recovery from his battle with COVID and was no longer in the hospital. Most people thought his would be the next funeral.

Though only about two hundred people stayed for the service, at least four hundred more came to the viewing to pay respects. It was a challenge for Quentin to attempt to recognize people wearing masks. The bishops were recognizable because of their gaudy robes and huge Super Bowl–sized episcopal rings. Others were recognized by distinctive voices that struck familiar chords in Quentin's memory. Still others, particularly the women, were recognizable by their flamboyant hats, which added color and pageantry to the proceedings. Quentin did not know many of the people who viewed the remains. His mother greeted everyone with a smile and the special dignity of a First Lady.

Quentin delivered a stirring eulogy that only a son could have given. His heart was heavy, and his soul moaned, but he had to represent his dad. He told stories of growing up as a preacher's kid and watching his father transform when he entered the pulpit. He shared several of the many lessons he had learned from his father, who loved to drop knowledge on anyone willing to listen. Quentin preached about a man of God who did all he could to lead God's people. He talked about a man with faults but a heart of gold and a desire to please the Lord. It was indeed a great homegoing celebration.

After the service was over, Quentin was exhausted. The Holy Spirit often drained him of his strength when he preached, and this was no exception. Before heading to the cemetery, he went to his office to change clothes and rest. He was shocked to find Mr. Alonzo Johnson sitting there. He was sharply dressed in a custom-made black windowpane suit and a matching black mask. His curly hair was impeccably styled.

"That was one great eulogy, young man," Johnson said. "I hope someone can preach over me like that when I get the call."

"Thank you, sir," Quentin said as he took his seat behind the desk. "But what are you doing here?"

"I told you that I knew your father and mother."

"No, I mean what are you doing *in my office*? I know you didn't come in here to collect money after my father's funeral."

Johnson closed his eyes and shook his head. "I came to thank you," he said softly.

Quentin was confused. "Thank me?"

"I remember when you laid hands on me and prayed in the hospital," Johnson said, clinching his lips and letting out a big breath. His eyes began to water. "I was in a bad way. I tried to ride the virus out at home, thinking couldn't no virus take out Mr. A. When I got to the hospital, they were whispering that I wasn't gonna make it." He shook his head. "And I agreed with'em. I ain't never been that sick." He choked up like he was about to cry. He reached into his pocket, pulled out a handkerchief, lifted his designer glasses, and dabbed his eyes.

"It was bad," Johnson said gently. "And then you came in the room out of nowhere, and when you touched me"—tears rolled down his face— "that changed everything. Something went through me that I had never felt in my life. It felt like you tazed me. Ain't that wild? But I knew at that moment I was healed. And all the bad numbers I had when I came into the hospital changed."

He took another deep breath. "Look, Rev. I've wreaked havoc in the lives of so many people. I've ruined families and marriages and closed countless businesses just because I had the power. I made lots of money, but I hurt many people along the way and didn't care. But when I tell you I saw the light." He stopped and shook his head. "It was… it was… a miracle." He began to sob.

"To God be the glory," Quentin said.

Johnson took a moment to collect himself. "So why did you do it?" he asked, peering through tear-filled eyes. "I was giving you a rough time, and I was threatening to harm your family and burn down your church. You could have let me die, and all your troubles would have been over. I don't get it."

Quentin searched for an explanation. "It was God. That's all I can say. I just caught a glimpse of you because I wasn't supposed to be in the hospital. But God tapped my brakes, and I had to pray for you."

"But I was your enemy."

"The Bible tells us to love our enemies," Quentin replied. "I wasn't going to let you die if I could help you, and I didn't care who you were. And God had already told me that somehow, we would pay you in full. I hope you see the lives of others a little differently now."

Johnson pulled down his mask to show Quentin a big smile. "I also came by to let you know that you can take all the time you need to repay the loan, and there will be no additional interest charges. And I am making a $50,000 donation to your church in the name of your father that I hope can be used to pay down the mortgage or help somebody." He reached into his pocket and laid an envelope on Quentin's desk.

"Are you serious?" Quentin asked.

"God and I had quite the conversation in the hospital room after you left. They put me in there to die. I know that. I promised God that if He allowed me to live, I would be a different, better man, and I plan to keep that promise. And it starts here, thanks to that divine touch that you gave me. And you didn't have to do it. Thank you for helping to turn my life around. Maybe I'll change my name to Paul." He smiled and laughed lightly.

"You know that changing how you live and do business is not going to be easy, right?" Quentin said. "You're really going to have to work on that. And with your reputation, it will not be easy."

"With God's help and a little assistance from my pastor"—he looked Quentin in the eyes— "I hope I can make it."

Quentin could sense the sincerity in his voice and saw a certain sparkle in his eyes. "Mr. Alonzo, I've got to go to the cemetery, but I want to thank you. And if you need anything, please don't hesitate to call me. And I hope you will be a regular at our services."

"I'll be there or online or wherever you have services. God's been too good." He stood up and stared Quentin in the eye. "You're gonna do great things here. Don't be discouraged by the contrarians and naysayers – do what God tells you to do." He patted his fist over his heart and walked out of the room.

Quentin's head was spinning, but he gave thanks to God.

A few days later, when they read Cornell's will, Quentin discovered that his father had left a $150,000 endowment to the church. He didn't know his father had that much cash. He also left money for Quentin, his granddaughters, and his wife. In the end, his estate was valued at close to $500,000.

"Momma, where did Pops get that kind of money?" Quentin asked.

"You know your father was as cheap as a Kmart suit," she said, cracking a smile. "He didn't spend no money. That's why we stayed in this tiny house all these years, even after he was prospering as a bishop. I didn't know he had *that much*, but he had money stashed in about six banks and credit unions. He had investments, and some of those pictures we have hanging on the walls are worth thousands. Who knew he was a financial genius?"

"What you gonna do now, Momma?"

"I'm gonna spend some of this money," she said. "In loving memory of my husband, of course."

CHAPTER 12

THE JOSHUA

F ive days after the reading of the will, Quentin got a call from the episcopal office. "Reverend Dillard, this is Sister Thelma. I am so sorry about your father's transition. He and I were close, you know."

"Thank you so much."

"I am calling because Bishop Jenkins needs to talk with you about an urgent matter. He wants to know when you will be available for a Zoom call. He's not getting around too much."

"I didn't think he was getting around at all," Quentin countered.

"It looked bad for a while, but we still serve a miracle-working God. Hallelujah. He is up, walking around, and even doing a little business. It is truly a miracle," Thelma said.

"I'm available whenever it is convenient to him. The bishop can call me any time."

Quentin had no idea what to expect during his call with Bishop Jenkins. Information had been quiet from the episcopal office for months. Quentin continued to operate as the pastor of Greater Faith after not hearing anything to the contrary. There were rumors on the pastoral rumor mill, but nothing was solid. Sister Thelma gave Quentin information for a Zoom call with Bishop Jenkins later that afternoon.

"How are you doing, son?" Jenkins began. "I know things must be difficult without your father."

Quentin noticed Bishop Jenkins's voice was not strong, and despite this being a Zoom call, the bishop did not turn on his camera.

"I'm doing fine, Bishop. Every day is challenging, but that was the case when my father was alive. I just have one less person to lean on. How are you doing? People are telling me that you are a walking talking miracle."

"I'm still on the road to recovery, but I'm doing much better than I was a month ago. I am a witness that the prayers of the righteous have tremendous power," he said. "I wanted to speak to you in confidence today because your father and I had unfinished business that I believe you can help me with."

"What business is that?" Quentin asked.

"Well, when your father was pastor, we had a, let me say, arrangement. He was supposed to tell you about it, but maybe he never had a chance."

"Exactly what arrangement are you talking about?"

There was a long silence. "It was a financial arrangement that was beneficial to us both."

Quentin's spirit began to tingle. He pressed the record button on his phone, sensing that this conversation was heading into a dark back alley.

"No, my father never mentioned any arrangement."

"Well, I'm sure you and your mother were surprised at the large sum of money your father had put away, I mean saved."

"What do you know about my father's finances?"

There was another long silence. "Quite often, bishops and selected pastors have a special agreement concerning the church's financial resources."

"What was *this* special agreement?"

"Before I explain it to you, I want you to know that this has been a common practice in the church for years. And it wasn't just your father but a group of pastors. It was our way of ensuring we had resources, especially those stuck in the antiquated payment arrangements of the church. I mean, who can survive on Pastor Appreciation Day, anniversaries, and birthdays, right?"

"I tried to change that payment system," Quentin said, "but I always got pushback from the church *and* the episcopal office."

"That is because there was already a workaround in place," Jenkins replied.

Quentin could feel the shade. "And exactly what is this *workaround*?"

"The pastors were advised to take 20 percent of each weekly offering as a set-aside. Sixty percent of that amount went to them, and 40 percent was reserved for their bishop."

Quentin had to do the math. "And the finance people didn't know about this?"

"In most cases, the pastor formed a partnership with the head of finance, who was rewarded. The point is that the pastors put this money in various accounts until the bishop requested his portion of the funds. According to my financing, your father had money set aside that was intended for my office."

"This doesn't sound legal, Bishop," Quentin said. "I mean, how can you take money from the church, and no one knows about it? That sounds like stealing to me."

"Hold on, young man," Jenkins said with a voice that suddenly found strength. "We were not stealing the money. As those called to lead, we are often asked to make difficult decisions. Sometimes for our congregations and other times for us. It's a fact, and we were only doing what should have been done."

Quentin wasn't buying any of the bishop's feeble explanation. "And exactly how much did my father have *intended* for you?"

There was silence and then whispering in the background. "According to my records, your father had about $40,000 set aside for the episcopal office."

Quentin hit the mute button. "You thieving son of a gun," he whispered.

He unmuted. "Bishop, I am so sorry. But my father provided detailed instructions for all the funds under his name. And there was not a $40,000 set-aside for you or your office."

There was more whispering. "Did you check the Joshua Fund?"

That name caught Quentin's attention. He remembered seeing that name in his father's stacks of paperwork but had no idea what it was for.

"I remember a reference to a Joshua Fund, but we never found any paperwork indicating any money anywhere. And I am a little confused, Bishop. Why would my father have a fund with such a large amount meant for you?"

"Look, Quentin. Your father was supposed to tell you all about this. It's no big deal. If you can locate the Joshua Fund, you will see plenty of money there for everyone."

"Let me do this, Bishop. Let me investigate this fund and meet with my finance committee to see…"

"Now, Quentin, this must be between you and me, just like your father and me. The fewer people who know, the fewer hands will be in the till. You know what I mean."

"Yeah, I know what you mean."

"Can I trust you with this, Quentin? I honestly believe you have a skyrocketing future at Greater Faith. The sky is the limit with the campus you have and the diversity you've built."

Quentin was getting tired of the flow of manure from Bishop Jenkins. "You continue to confuse me, Bishop. The last time we had a real conversation, you tried to remove me from the church. Now, with a mysterious $40,000 on the line, I'm the next great pastor in the denomination. You must be eating fish tonight. I can smell it over the telephone."

"Quentin, I'm not feeling well. I need you to find the Joshua Fund, and there will probably be documentation to show that a portion of the money in the fund was intended for me. Check the

Regency Credit Union in Fairfield. Please get back to me when you find something. And again, let's keep this between us. No one needs to know. I'll call you in a few days."

When he logged off ZOOM, Quentin's stomach felt like it was going to explode. He sat quietly to absorb all the information Bishop Jenkins gave him. He didn't know what to think or do, and he knew that the key was the Joshua Fund, whatever that was. He decided to visit his mother to see if she knew anything about it.

Quentin's parents' house seemed colder than normal when he walked into the front of the house. He paused to look at several of the Charles Bibbs paintings on the walls and could hardly believe they were worth thousands of dollars. As he made his way into the kitchen, he was surprised that the lights were not on, and no food was cooking. His mother was in her familiar place at the kitchen table, seemingly staring at the television that was not on. Her hair was in a dark blue bonnet, and she wore her red flannel bathrobe.

"I keep waiting for him to get out of the chair or at least ask for some sweet tea he knew he couldn't have," she said, stirring her tea slowly. "I knew he was sick. And I knew I would probably outlive him. But this doesn't seem right. Nothing seems right."

"You all right, Momma?" Quentin asked.

She looked at him like she didn't realize he was in the room. "Well, it's about time you came to see about your mother."

"Momma, I have talked to you every day for the past two weeks."

"Talking ain't seeing," she said. "I could be wasting away to nothing, and as long as I had a strong voice, you wouldn't know anything about it."

"That's because you refuse to use FaceTime, which I have shown you how to do numerous times."

"I ain't using FaceTime. I *want* face time. Y'all gotta come see me. I ain't no face-on-the-phone momma."

"OK. I am here now, and it is good to see you."

She looked at Quentin and smiled. "It's good to see you too, baby. Now what you want? My show is getting ready to come on. And I know Steve Harvey gonna be lookin' good today."

"You still watchin' Family Feud?"

"Every night and every day. Even your father knew that Steve Harvey was my second love. And why are you here?"

"I recently had a very interesting conversation with Bishop Jenkins."

"I thought he was dead."

"No. He was very sick. But miraculously, it appears he has recovered."

"What is he talking about? I never did trust him," she said. "He's as slippery as an ice rink."

"Do you know anything about a Joshua Fund that Pops might have had?" Quentin asked.

Essie gave him a strange look. "The only thing Joshua I know about is that hideous award your father won a few years back. It's in his office. That thing should have met the garbageman years ago, but your father loved that ugly thing."

"What was it for?"

"Some mysterious award given him by members of the episcopal board. It had something to do with leading people to the promised land. I would have let that monstrosity lead me to the garbage dump."

"It can't be that bad."

"Go on in there and see. But brace yourself."

Quentin had not been in his father's office in more than a decade. It was Cornell's private domain. The door had a lock, and his father had the only key.

"Is the office unlocked?" Quentin asked.

"I guess so. I haven't stepped foot in there for twenty years," his mother said. "I don't know what might be in there. If I came close to going in, Cornell would start barking like a rabid dog."

The office was in the rear of the house, away from everything else. As Quentin walked down the hallway, he felt like a time traveler. He was surprised when he turned the doorknob to the office and found it unlocked. He entered slowly and carefully, halfway expecting to hear his father's objection: *"Boy, you know you can't come in here without permission."*

Quentin peered into the room like a child going where he was not supposed to go. The pictures on the wall and the fading traces of cigar smoke stirred a bevy of memories. As he pushed the door open, he smiled when he saw the four large bookshelves that lined the office's back wall. The shelves were packed with Bibles, commentaries, Bible dictionaries, and a plethora of theology books from many of his father's favorite authors, including Dietrich Bonhoeffer, Jürgen Moltmann, Howard Thurman, Martin Luther King Jr, and Tony Evans.

Quentin did not realize he had not taken a step into the office. He stood frozen at the door.

"Well, are you going to go in?" his mother asked, standing at the far end of the hallway. "He ain't gonna bite you."

Quentin did not acknowledge his mother as he slowly stepped into the office. It was dark with the lights off and the blinds closed, but this was familiar territory. When he was a child, he would come into this office and visit his father. They had great times playing games, singing, and watching sports on the small black-and-white television that was painted in dust in the corner.

When he turned on the light, the room seemed to come alive. Memories sat comfortably in each corner and on every shelf. Quentin could not help but smile as he remembered the good times with his father in this space. Nothing had changed. There were a few newer pictures of the family on the desk, but the same off-green wallpaper screamed from the walls. Pictures of his father with numerous bishops and celebrities had found their homes in old wooden frames meticulously organized around the room. This was his father's place of peace.

"Well, do you see the ugly thing?" his mother asked.

Quentin turned and looked behind the door to see a large

contraption that seemed to know it was the ugliest piece in the room. He stared at the creation, which needed to explain itself. The design was two feet of utter metallic confusion resembling a vertical rollercoaster ride with twisted and jagged tracks. It reminded Quentin of surrealist art he saw at the museum that had a different meaning to everyone who looked at it. The caption on the large wooden base read: *We've Come This Far By Faith.* Quentin took several steps back and to the side to get a different point of view, but nothing locked in or brought Joshua to mind. He was utterly confused. He tried to lift it, but it must have weighed more than a hundred pounds.

"How long are you gonna be in there?" his mother called out. "What are you doing, moving in?"

"I'm examining the Joshua award," Quentin replied.

"I hope you enjoy examining ugly," she replied. "I can't tell you how many times I wanted to sneak in there and throw that thing away."

"I'm glad you didn't try. This thing is heavy."

Quentin began inspecting the award carefully. He turned on the flashlight on his cellphone and noticed a variety of inscriptions engraved on various parts of the tracks. Some were scriptures, and the others were dates. Once he saw his father's birthday and several other dates he recognized, he realized this was a life map. Significant dates in his father's life were inscribed, including the day he got married, the date of his initial ordination, the opening day of Greater Faith, his wedding anniversary, and Quentin's birthday. The twists and turns of the tracks represented the ups and downs of life's journey. There were scriptures and Greek words along the jagged path.

Then he saw the critical phrase: *For the Lord, your God is with you wherever you go.* Joshua 1:9b.

The tracks led him to the rear of the award, which had a drawer and a built-in six-digit combination lock. Quentin had to close the office door to position himself to figure out the combination. He put in every birthday he could think of but to no avail. Then he began applying key dates on the award. Nothing worked. He laughed when he saw the words "Bible Feud" engraved near the end of the track. That was an old code-word game he and his father played frequently. With that clue in mind, he took the final two digits of the last three scriptures on the award, and the drawer popped open. Inside was an envelope with Quentin's name on it, which was a little eerie. The letter sat on top of a small, worn notebook.

Quentin could not believe the letter, but he knew his father had understood that he was the only one who could open the Joshua. He just stared at the words on the page, utterly astonished. Then he opened the notebook, which turned out to be a ledger. He had to sit at his father's desk to absorb all that he was reading. There were no names but initials and lots of numbers. Once he realized what was going on, his heart began beating rapidly. He sat at the desk with his hand covering his mouth.

Oh my God, he thought.

CHAPTER 13

THE BOARD OF BISHOPS

After about an hour of contemplation, Quentin came out of the office dazed. His mother was sitting at the kitchen table, sipping her tea.

"Did you get what you need?" she asked before looking at her son. "My goodness. Did you see a ghost in there?"

"I saw more than I needed to see, I'll tell you that."

"More than you needed to see. Your father wasn't hiding pornography in there, was he?"

"Momma? No."

"I had to ask," she said. "He spent a lot of quiet time in there, and I didn't know what he was doing."

"I think I know what he was doing. Now there is something *I* need to do."

"Are you going to tell me what's going on?"

"No, Momma, I am not. All I can give you are the words of a song: you'll understand it better by and by."

After rereading the letter and carefully examining the ledger, Quentin had no choice but to arrange a meeting with Bishop Jenkins. He told the bishop that his father had set aside $50,000 for him. The bishop was elated and quickly agreed to the meeting. Quentin insisted they meet at the episcopal office.

"For this kind of meeting, I think we should be as far from HQ as possible," Jenkins said. "The fewer people who see us together, the better."

"I have to go to HQ to drop off a package pertaining to my father's benefits and insurance," Quentin replied. "If I'm going to be there, we can take care of our business too. Especially since the offices are about halfway for both of us."

"All right, all right. We'll meet at HQ, but we need to arrive at different times and not tell anyone why we are meeting. You got that?"

"Oh, I'm very clear about that," Quentin replied.

"Do you have cash or a check?" Jenkins asked.

"What's best for you?"

"I am not exactly looking for a clear paper trail here. If you can get the cash, do that."

"That's a lot of cash," Quentin said. "I am not comfortable carrying around that much cheese. I'll probably have to get a cashier's check."

On the day of the appointment, Quentin traveled ninety miles to the episcopal office, arriving an hour before the meeting with Bishop Jenkins. He found Thelma Hudson's executive office at the rear of the large, single-story building that looked like it had been an elementary school. When he walked in, her eyes lit up.

"You must be Rev. Dillard. My goodness, you look like your father, even with your mask on."

"You recognize me because I look like my dad?"

"Well, I'll admit that he had shown me pictures of you. He was so proud of all you accomplished. But what are you doing here so early?" she asked. "Bishop Jenkins told me you were coming and that he would meet you in one of the private offices. But you're not supposed to be here for another hour."

"I came by to visit with you," Quentin said with a smile.

Thelma did not look like he imagined. She was probably in her late sixties and wore a long black wig without a trace of gray hair. Her sizeable red-and-black glasses framed her face and complimented her ruby red lipstick, which looked like a fluorescent stop sign. She had a sawdust-colored complexion, and her makeup was hard at work covering a series of bumps, freckles, and traces of a mustache that she could not hide.

Thelma smiled uncomfortably. "Please have a seat. And exactly why do you want to visit with me?"

"Well, I know that you and my father had a relationship of some kind, and I wanted to talk to you about it."

"Now, it's nothing like that," she said. "I just really admired your father. When we had episcopal meetings in cities around the country, we always had dinner together at least one night. He was the funniest little man. And so smart."

For the next twenty minutes, Thelma shared stories about her adventures with Quentin's father. Some were funny and others she didn't need to share, but it was apparent she knew his father well.

"And what about the rumor?" Quentin asked.

Thelma adjusted her glasses and shifted in her chair. "What rumor are you talking about?"

"The one where you told people that you slept with my father at one of those meetings. And the rumor you threatened to spread if my father didn't provide certain favors."

Thelma's face contorted, and the atmosphere in her office seemed to shift. "I don't know what you are talking about," she snapped. "And your accusations are insulting, slanderous, and baseless."

"I've got it all in writing," Quentin replied confidently.

"Well, someone was writing lies. I don't know what you are talking about."

"Now you're calling my recently deceased father a liar because he wrote everything down. All the details."

They stared at each other like venomous snakes preparing to attack. Just then, Bishop Jenkins came through the door.

"What are all the cars doing here?" he asked.

"What cars are you talking about?" Thelma asked.

"The parking lot is almost full. Is there another meeting scheduled today?"

Thelma looked through her calendar. "No. Absolutely nothing is going on."

Bishop Jenkins had a strange look on his face. "Something is absolutely going on. I don't know what it is, but it don't feel right." He looked at Quentin. "You know anything about this?"

As Quentin was composing a response, Bishop Malachi Wilson came to the door. Wilson was the chairperson of the episcopal board. Bishop Jenkins and Thelma looked like they were staring at a ghost. And not the Holy Ghost.

"Bishop Wilson," Jenkins said, forcing a smile. "What are you doing here?"

"I'd like for all three of you to come with me to the main boardroom," Wilson said.

Bishop Jenkins looked at Thelma, who shook her head, indicating she did not know what was going on. Then he glared at Quentin, who rolled his eyes and stood up. Wilson turned and walked toward the boardroom.

"What have you done, Quentin?" Jenkins barked.

"I guess you'll see in a minute," Quentin replied.

"Excuse me, Bishop Wilson. I need to go to the bathroom. I'll be in the boardroom in just a minute," Thelma said, smiling brightly.

Wilson proceeded through a maze of halls before reaching the boardroom. Six bishops from across the country were seated at the large table when they walked in. Jenkins looked like he had entered the last place he wanted to be.

"Please come in and have a seat. Reverend Jenkins, you sit here," Wilson said.

Quentin had never appeared before the bishops' board, which

was good. He had met the collection of the highest-ranking officers in the denomination at his father's funeral. There were nine bishops on the board, six men and three women. This morning, seven bishops sat socially distanced around the large table with two other bishops on a large screen behind the chairperson. Each bishop present was impeccably dressed. The men wore custom-made dark suits, either navy blue or black. Five of the six men wore flashy bowties. Bishop Margaret Mackall wore a red African print suit that was simply stunning. The two other female bishops were dressed in navy blue business suits. All the bishops wore their special pin and bishop rings. Quentin nearly laughed when he noticed the amount of black hair dye on almost every head in the room. The age of the bishops ranged from late sixties to early eighties. The smell of multiple perfumes and colognes with a tinge of liniment battled in the air.

The boardroom was breathtaking. Anchored by the large cherry wood table, the oval room had pictures of every bishop who had served the CFC on its sky-blue walls, which were accented by white picture frame molding. The mission statement of the denomination—Praising God, Equipping People, Making Disciples—was printed on one wall. Each bishop sat in an oversized black leather chair, and their assistants sat behind them. A large gold-and-crystal chandelier, almost the length of the eighteen-foot table, lit the room.

"Reverend Dillard, you are not allowed to sit at the bishops table, but please take one of the seats on the outer wall," Wilson said.

After a few moments of silence, Bishop Jenkins spoke up. "Bishops, it is good to see all of you. I certainly hope you are not here because of the little conflict Reverend Dillard and I recently had at his church. I assure you that everything is rectified. My life has changed since my bout with COVID. Old things have passed away. So, there is really no need to have this meeting."

Wilson gave Jenkins a stern look. "That is *not* why we are here. We have heard about that unfortunate incident, but we are meeting this morning on a much more serious matter." He looked around. "Where is our episcopal secretary?"

The room's door opened. One of the security guards entered, holding tightly to Thelma's arm. "She was making a run for it just like you said she might," the guard said with a grin. "But she wasn't getting out of here on my watch."

Thelma had transformed into a horrid-looking creature. Her wig was pulled to the side, her glasses were lopsided, her clothes were disheveled, and her mask only covered her chin. She wore a scowl that would strike fear into a pack of hungry wolves. It looked like she and the guard had gotten into quite a tussle.

"Sit down, Sister Thelma," Wilson commanded.

She tried to collect herself, pulling her mask over her nose and taking her seat. "Do you need me to take notes, Bishop?" she asked politely while breathing deeply.

"No. I need you to listen to the charges that have been levied against you and Reverend Jenkins." Wilson reached into his briefcase, pulled out Bishop Dillard's ledger, and placed it on the table.

"Oh, snap," Thelma said and then turned to shoot a laser glare at Quentin. "Oh, excuse me," she said, being careful not to make eye contact with any of the bishops.

Jenkins looked at the ledger, closed his eyes, and slowly dropped his head.

"I believe you now know why we are here, Reverend Jenkins. According to this ledger and a letter left by the late Bishop Cornell Dillard, you and Sister Thelma have been involved in a rather large scheme that has cheated churches out of tens of thousands of dollars over the past five years. This is unacceptable behavior for a bishop in our church and a high-ranking administrative officer. I had to pray to see if I was going to call this meeting or call the police because what is recorded here is felony theft, and I am afraid someone may have to do jail time."

Jenkins stood up slowly. "This scheme was Sister Thelma's from the very beginning," he said.

"Sit down and shut up, you old goat!" she yelled.

Wilson hammered his gavel. "Reverend Jenkins, sit down. And

Sister Thelma, if you have one more outburst like that at *this* table, you will be removed... in handcuffs. Do you understand?"

Quentin sat stunned at the rear of the room.

Jenkins started coughing and reached for one of the water pitchers on the table.

Wilson continued, "Bishop Dillard took extensive notes on every transaction you two have overseen and the eight churches involved. Interestingly, most of those churches have new pastors, who, after an interview, thought this was how we did business." Wilson glared at Jenkins and Thelma.

"You are a disgrace to our denomination and our God. And Sister Thelma, it does seem you are the architect of this sinful thievery. You're fired. And you need to thank God that we are not pressing charges, but you will have to pay the board a lot of money back. You will be getting a visit from our legal representatives. Now please, pack your office because you should not be here when this meeting is over."

"You're not going to let me say anything?" she protested. "I have a simple explanation. This was all the work of Bishop Dillard. He did it all and arranged the books to frame me. I never did like that man."

Wilson shook his head like he was absorbing Thelma's response. "It is so interesting that Bishop Dillard wrote in his letter to this board that you would accuse him because he would not be here to respond to your accusations. I believe the bishop. You were fired just about thirty seconds ago. Enough said." Wilson signaled to the security officer, who tapped Thelma on the shoulder.

"Touch me again, rent-a-cop, and I'll cut you five ways to Sunday." She stood up and stormed out of the room.

There was a long silence. "Now we must deal with you, Reverend Jenkins. Do you have anything to say?"

Jenkins stood up slowly. "First, giving honor to my Lord and Savior Jesus Christ as I stand before this distinguished gathering of the finest theological minds in this country. I am at your mercy. I have

sinned and fallen short. I am just a man, and I ask for forgiveness."
He paused, looking around the room. "The Bible says—"

"We all know what the Bible says, Reverend Jenkins," Wilson
snapped. "And you should have already perceived that we have
forgiven you to some degree, or you would be going to jail. So don't
push it."

Jenkins smiled and coughed slightly. "Forgive me, sir. If that is
the case, I guess I should thank the board for your compassion, and
I ask that you pray for me that I might someday return to the leader
of men God called me to be. I throw myself on the mercy of this
body." He sat down and continued coughing.

Wilson took a deep breath. Quentin could feel the uneasiness
in the room. Several of the bishops were wiping their eyes. Others
were praying, clinching their hands. Obviously, this was a difficult
moment for the board.

"First, I hope you noticed that I did not call you *Bishop* Jenkins
because this board has voted to defrock you," Wilson said. "And you
will not be allowed to pastor or speak at a church in our denomination
for the next five years. In addition, you will place back in the coffers
of this denomination the sum of $150,000. And just so you know,
Bishop Dillard, who admitted his reluctant participation in this
scheme, sent us the money he took before he passed away."

"Is there anything anyone on the board would like to say as we
close out this gathering?" Wilson asked.

Bishop Wendall Richardson raised his hand. He was the oldest
member of the board, serving as a bishop for more than sixteen
years. "We have been rather silent this morning, but for the record,
I want it to be known that this is an extremely sad day for this board
and our denomination," he said. "I have been in the church more
than seventy-five years, and nothing close to this has ever happened.
This may never reach the news, and I certainly hope it does not,
but we owe our congregations an apology for how we, as leaders,
allowed this to happen. And Reverend Jenkins, your behavior here
is appalling. And I want you to know how close the vote was to turn

you over to the police. I would ask now that we pray for this body, our denomination, Reverend Jenkins, Sister Thelma, and all who have been a part of this. We need help from our Lord today and moving forward."

As Richardson concluded his prayer, which blended sadness, poetry and divine power, there was not a sound in the room. Most of the bishops had their heads down, and Wilson looked ready to start a fight.

"Is there anything you would like to say, Reverend Dillard, since you brought us this evidence?" Wilson asked.

Quentin did not want to speak, but something on the inside prompted him to stand and stare at Reverend Jenkins. He then turned to address the body. "Bishop Wilson, this has been an excruciating process. Learning about this scheme and my father's role in it is very disheartening. After recently burying my father and having many sick and dying people in our churches turns my stomach. I have to wonder if I am meant to be in this denomination. Your leadership during this pandemic has been pathetic. We heard nothing. And when you decided, you came into our churches, making us keep our doors open in extremely dangerous times. Now you have bishops and a leadership team member stealing money from churches. This is terrible. This is newsworthy. Our people need to know."

"This is a close-house item. Nothing we have discussed here can be discussed outside of these walls," Wilson said. "Those are the rules."

"That's not right," Quentin said. "The people have the right to know what the leadership is doing with their money and disciplinary actions taken on their behalf. The people must know."

"No one has complained," Bishop Johnnie Jordan said.

Quentin looked at the highfaluting bishops around the table. "I'm complaining," he said with attitude. "And I know I wouldn't be alone if the news got out."

"What happens in our meetings will not get out," Wilson said.

"What happens here *shouldn't* get out, but this type of scandalous information gets leaked all the time," Quentin said.

Wilson looked at the bishops around the table. "Reverend Dillard, we're going to ask you to leave the room while we discuss this matter. We will call you back in a few minutes. Thank you."

As he stood to leave the room, glares from several bishops should have melted Quentin like candle wax. But he was tired of all the cloak-and-dagger and mysterious manipulations from this board. His father had talked about it a lot, and now he understood.

After a few minutes, which Quentin spent in prayer, he was asked back into the room.

"Exactly what do you want?" Wilson asked.

"I no longer want this body to be a secret organization," Quentin began. "There has got to be some transparency. I know some issues discussed among the bishops are confidential, but *everything* can't be. We need to know what the bishops are planning. We need to hear from our bishops in times of crisis. The pastors and even congregants should have open communication with this body. Ain't no telling what y'all are doing, really. I know we send money to the episcopal office every month. And I am told that each of you is on salary, but you won't allow the churches to have a salary arrangement with the pastors. How can we live comfortably depending on three or four fundraising events? We, the pastors of the CFC, want salaries, benefits, expense accounts, and a housing allowance. And we need more women pastors too."

The bishops seemed uneasy.

"Is that all, Reverend Dillard?" Wilson asked.

"That's not all, but it's a good start. We are just looking for some equity here and a better understanding of our direction, which I believe is supposed to come from you."

"We will take your request under consideration," Wilson said. "You need to give them to us in writing in the next thirty days."

Quentin couldn't believe his ears. "Thirty days," he barked. "Y'all just stalling. I recorded my previous statement and can have my request to you in five minutes. If you try to sweep this under the rug with stall tactics, what happened here today will be front-page news. I guarantee you that."

"Reverend Dillard, we have entered your request into the official minutes of this organization, and we will begin moving on them immediately," Wilson said. "To be honest, we have been discussing a more equitable financial solution for our pastors, and we will move on that. And when we hire our new episcopal secretary, we will become a more transparent organization. Does that meet your demands?"

"Y'all are notoriously slow at doing anything," Quentin said, looking at each bishop at the table. "I want to set deadlines for these changes and immediately draft and release a letter to all the pastors letting them know the changes to expect in the next two months."

Quentin sat down, amazed at the confrontational tone that had sprouted during his time with the bishops. He had come to this meeting with no intention of challenging the bishops' board, but years of frustration as a pastor bore the fruit of his words. He spoke from his heart and hoped changes would happen.

CHAPTER 14

❖

RETURN TO THE TEMPLE

After a few days, Bishop Wilson called Quentin to inform him that he appreciated his honesty and that many of the changes he had recommended to the board of bishops were being implemented. Wilson also told Quentin that he was officially recognized as the senior pastor of Greater Faith. In a surprising move, Wilson wanted Quentin to become an advisor to the board to help improve communications with pastors and churches.

The word spread quickly about Quentin's episcopal confrontation. He became a folk hero to the 278 pastors in the denomination. Pastors throughout the CFC were calling to thank him for his efforts.

"Doc, just want to thank you, man," Pastor Marlon Brown said during a call. "For the first time in ten years, I have hope that I will be put on salary and not have to try to survive on anniversaries and birthdays. That's a big step. You've got all the pastors beaming."

"It's the first step," Quentin responded.

"It's a great step," Brown added. "Thanks so much."

For Quentin, the meeting with the bishops and the subsequent ramifications briefly overshadowed the effects of the COVID virus, which was still infecting people in the church and community. Two

COVID-19 vaccines were approved, and distribution plans were being implemented, but no one knew how long the rollout would take.

Quentin saw an opportunity to use several of the larger buildings on the Greater Faith campus as vaccination sites. He called the county health department and volunteered the use of the church's facilities. He told them that people of color would be more trusting if the shots were given at a church.

"Pastor, we thank you so much, but no one has mentioned using churches yet," one of the administrators said.

"Well, you need to let the county planning committee know they will have difficulty getting Black people to take any vaccine. You're going to need some trusted community partners. In fact, you will need a whole campaign about safety, trust, and reliability."

"Thank you so much for your ideas," the administrator said. "I'll bring your suggestions before the board at our next meeting."

After two more weeks, Quentin was pleased to see the number of infections and deaths decrease across the county. Government officials were loosening the restrictions and allowing churches to open at 25 percent capacity. That meant two hundred people would be allowed at the Greater Faith service if Quentin decided to open the church. He received mixed messages from his leadership and congregants. Some were anxious to gather for worship, while others were comfortable watching or listening from the comfort of their homes. There was still a lot of fear, even with the vaccine. No one knew what to expect at the church, but they knew their homes were safe.

"Pastor, I'm gonna be truthful with you," said Gloria Smith during one of the pastor's calls. "I ain't trying to get around a whole lot of people. Ain't no way to know who got the vaccine, and we don't know who got the rona. Those aceramic people, or whatever they're called, may have it and spread it to everybody. I love my God and my church, but I won't be coming in that building until I am one hundred percent certain I won't get sick."

"Sister Smith, you weren't 100 percent safe before rona," Quentin countered.

"Well, I won't be making that mistake this time."

Even Deacon Justice, who had been adamant about not closing the church, was hesitant to return. "Pastor, I've had six people in my family get the virus, and two died. They don't even know how they got it. A few months ago, I didn't think it was real, so I thought closing the church was foolish. But now, I think we should stay closed for the rest of the year to ensure this thing's spread is under control. Or maybe we should only let fully vaccinated people come to the live service. We can't be too careful."

"But I thought you said we were not meant to have church over the internet," Quentin responded.

"Well, you get older, and you *should* get wiser," Justice replied. "I'll admit I was wrong about that. The services have been different, but the spirit of the Lord has been with us."

"Wow, I thought you'd be the first one running through the door," Quentin said.

"Pastor, that's not a race I'm trying to win. I'm sure I'll come back, but I ain't in no hurry."

After reviewing a survey completed by members of the congregation, Quentin set a date for the grand reopening of the church. He knew everyone was not coming back right away, but he wanted to begin the return process, which would take place in six weeks to correspond with the forty-fifth anniversary of the church.

To his surprise, the board of bishops sent a correspondence to all the pastors advising them to follow the directions of their states and counties as they prepared to reopen. Quentin shared his ideas for the opening with his worship design team and left it in their hands. His challenge was to spread the word that Greater Faith would have two services on that Sunday morning using the main sanctuary and the small chapel. Quentin held a Zoom meeting with his leadership team to unveil his reopening vision.

"Are there any questions?" Quentin asked after providing the details for the reopening celebration.

"Let's be real, Pastor Q. The question is if anybody is coming," Deacon Jasper Johnson said. "We've been devastated these last eighteen months. I ain't never seen so much sickness and never known so many people die in a short period of time. We're starting to come out of it, but some people are still not ready to leave their homes. This COVID fear, even with the vaccine coming, is still alive and well."

"Don't you think people are ready to return to church?" Quentin asked. "If any place should lead the way in coming back and doing it right, it should be us. I know people are still scared, but it will be up to us to help turn their fear into joy because everyone present knows God did something special in their lives. We have to celebrate the sunshine *and* the rain."

"Pastor Q, you know I've always been real with you. I've been at Greater Faith for twelve years and been with you since the beginning," said Maceo Greene. "But I ain't coming back for a while. I've got preexisting respiratory issues, and I can't risk my health. When you see as many saints as we saw die from this thing, we have to wonder if God is giving us any special covering."

"I have prayed about this, and I believe it's time," Quentin said adamantly. "God is ready to welcome us back, as long as we learned something along the way."

Sarah Jackson chimed in. "I learned that many people died, good people, saints of God. I learned that all the prayers in the world couldn't keep the people very close to you from getting sick and dying."

"I know you're hurting, Sister Sarah, but you might want to look at it another way," Quentin said. "Understand that even in death, God has a plan. It hurts and seems unfair, but none of us are getting out of this thing called life alive. You're still here. The memories of the loved ones you lost are still with you. So what are you going to do? Stay angry with God? Walk away from your calling?"

Quentin paused and then continued, "Walking with this cross is not easy. The Bible tells us that. We are not spared from suffering, pain, or anguish, just as Jesus was not spared. But we must understand that through it all, God is with us. Know that God's ways are not our ways, and in the end, we will be victorious. Our calling is to have faith and believe."

Quentin listened to the views of a few more of his leadership team before summarizing how he would move forward. He truly felt their pain. Greater Faith had lost more than a dozen people to the virus, and the connections with others who were lost reached into the thirties. People were hurting and afraid. Quentin knew his responsibility was to convince his congregants that even in this they must trust God.

"I know many of you are not on board with opening the church, and I ask that you pray for us as we move forward. Pray that we are doing God's will," Quentin said. "Pray that we will be able to keep everyone safe moving forward. And pray that we will see God's vision and not be afraid to walk into it, sooner rather than later. This is about faith. Do we believe that God is with us? If we truly believe, we must move forward knowing that God is on our side."

Time passed quickly, and to Quentin's delight, he received fewer calls about infections, hospitalizations, and deaths from the virus. He continued to ask that members of the congregation get their vaccinations if only to help keep others safe. After three weeks, the county finally asked to use Greater Faith as a vaccination site, and they served more than a thousand people in one week. Quentin did get a few calls from people who'd had a bad reaction to the vaccine, but he took it all in stride.

The reopening was only a few days away, but Quentin could not get details from his worship design team, a group he trusted. He and the team had worked together to produce outstanding services for more than five years. He wondered why he was intentionally being kept out of the loop, but he was told to focus on God's word for the day, and they would do the rest.

Quentin called his mother to see if she planned to attend the grand reopening.

"I am prayin' on that one," his mother said, "'cause I don't believe all them people gonna be safe. I'm fully vaccinated, but unless we check vaccination cards at the door, there's gonna be somebody in there praisin' God full of the rona."

"But you felt safe when people came to church with the flu."

"They shoulda stayed their sick tails at home too," she replied. "But I never really thought about the danger. Moving forward, if anyone coughs or sneezes, they should get dragged out of the church and put in isolation."

"Momma, if you're vaccinated, you're covered. And everyone in the church will be asked to keep their mask on."

"You know good and well Mother Amy is not gonna keep that mask on. When she gets happy and starts shoutin', she can hardly keep her clothes on… She lost a lotta weight, you know."

"Well, make up your mind. I would love to see you there."

Quentin woke up early on the morning of the reopening service and spent extra time in prayer. He felt God had given him a good word for the service, but not knowing what would be happening worried him. As he prayed, he received a revelation that made him laugh. It was all a setup. His worship team was doing something special they did not want him to know about. He wondered what the service would look like, but he felt in his spirit it would be an extraordinary day.

Quentin arrived at the church about an hour before the service was scheduled to begin, and there were only a few cars in the parking lot. Inside the church, the trustees, were making sure everything was in place. The ushers, masked and nattily dressed, were meeting to discuss how they would handle the crowd. He talked to a few people until about thirty minutes before the service was to start, and the sanctuary was basically empty.

"Sister Jones, is anyone coming today?" Quentin asked.

"We'll see, Pastor Q. We're all praying that a few people will be brave enough to come out."

Quentin was discouraged as he made his way to his office at the rear of the church. He heard voices telling him the service would be a disaster with only a few people in the sanctuary. After arriving in his office, he played gospel music on his iPad and began to pray. After he was assured that the service was in God's hands, he put on his robe and prepared for a live worship service for the first time in more than a year. He was joined by members of his ministerial staff for a final joint prayer.

"Is anyone out there?" Quentin asked.

"Pastor, the picking's are slim," Deacon Jones said. "But the Bible says where two or three are gathered, so we're all good."

Quentin felt like an anvil had been tied to his heart when he walked into the sanctuary. There were only about twenty people scattered in the space, which typically held five hundred. He immediately thought he had made a mistake opening the church, but he heard the voice asking, *Where is your faith?* He personally greeted the few people in the sanctuary, all wearing masks, and they seemed genuinely happy to be in church and to see their pastor.

Quentin was asked to take his seat in the pulpit so the service could begin. He didn't see the need for such a protocol because there were so few people in the sanctuary. His head was pounding as he went to the chancellor's area and asked the Lord's will to be done. As he sat down, Tony sat proudly on the B3 organ and began playing as the door to the main aisle opened.

Members of the church band dashed into place and began playing, "I Was Glad When They Said Unto Me." Liturgical dancers flowed through the doors and down the middle aisle. They were masked, dressed in a rainbow of colors, dancing, clapping, and leaping. Then the choir came through the doors in stunning lavender robes, singing with angelic voices that seemed to lift the roof of the building.

Quentin had to stand and give God thanks as tears welled in his eyes. He had missed this harmony and power for more than a year. But this was something extra. The choir marched in rhythm, singing to the glory of the Lord. There was clapping and tambourines. Oh, they were singing. Members of all the church's choirs were a part of this ensemble. As they reached the choir stand, Sister Carretha took the microphone and wailed to the heavens. *My God can she sing*, he thought.

When he turned his attention back to the middle aisle, he was shocked to see Sister Harriett slowly entering the sanctuary. She was among many who held a black flag with the words "Heaven Bound" written on it. Her husband, Brother Frank, had fought a good fight but never recovered from COVID-19 and eventually died. Behind her were Adembe and Shalela, bouncing and dancing while holding the twins. Quentin spotted Mr. Alonzo praising at the rear of the church. Cedric Boyd, or whoever he was, marched in like a proud soldier. Quentin smiled brightly beneath his mask as Todd and his family came down the main aisle, trying desperately to find the beat. They, too, were dressed in African attire.

Everyone who came in wore a mask, including a few custom-made masks that matched their outfits. The musical medley continued to modulate. Tears flowed as the procession of old friends and familiar faces came through the door. No one was just walking; they were rocking to the beat, singing, clapping, bobbing their heads, and waving their hands. Those who had recovered from COVID waved colorful flags that read "Healed: COVID-Free."

The doors to the two outer aisles opened, and more people pranced in. It was an amazing procession. Quentin loved to see the older saints strut. It was a scene he would never forget. Hundreds of people came in, undoubtedly exceeding the county's limitations, but they came to praise God. Quentin was informed that there were also people in the church's small chapel who were watching the service.

The ushers did their best to socially distance the congregants, but it was a challenging assignment.

After a few minutes of uninterrupted escalating praise, the doors closed, and the band stopped playing. The lights in the sanctuary were lowered as the choir began singing, "I Just Want to Praise Him." Quentin did not fight the tears. He smiled brightly, knowing this was his mother's favorite song. Then the main door opened, and everyone stood.

His mother appeared at the door, dressed in a stunning white silk dress that flowed to her ankles. Her white shoes glittered, and her white bedazzled hat was so big he wondered if she would make it through the door. She wore black gloves, symbolizing her mourning at the loss of her husband, but she looked extraordinary. Everyone applauded as she pranced down the middle aisle, looking like the Queen Mother. Vanessa and the girls followed her. Quentin could not stop the tears. He only wished his father could be there to see this. His mother came to her seat on the front row and winked at her son. *She knew all along*, he thought. The choir kept modulating, and the people loved the praise. Quentin was in divine ecstasy. People were spaced out on the main floor, and in the balcony seats, everyone was praising. He felt like this was a precursor to heaven.

The worship design team had planned an awesome service that included a tribute to all those who died or were infected by COVID-19. They also did a special tribute to Bishop Cornell Dillard and presented a plaque naming the sanctuary after the church's founder.

The worship service exceeded Quentin's wildest expectations. He looked at members of his worship design team, seated together, and bowed his head, showing his approval and respect for their labor. He was so filled with the joy of the Holy Spirit that he almost forgot he had to preach. Overflowing with divine energy, Quentin brought the word with fervor under the sermon title, "Ain't No Stopping Us Now."

Quentin preached with power, passion, and joy. Having the

congregation engage in call and response during the sermon took him to another level. Brother Todd worked the organ, providing chord after elevating chord, which Quentin used like stairs to climb closer to heaven. Quentin dropped several theological nuggets that caused worshiping hands to rise and more than a few people stood to their feet. He walked down the stairs toward the congregation, talking to them like he knew their every thought and need. He bobbed, twisted, and turned; the physical nature of his sermon delivery was mind-blowing. Sweat streamed down his face, but it didn't stop his flow. Quentin was on fire. Amens and hallelujahs rained in the church like a spring storm in the Congo rainforest. Mother Amy started shouting and quickly lost her mask, as Quentin's mother had predicted. In a familiar scene, Sister Paul began to shout like a whirling dervish, holding her dress with one hand and her wig with another.

Once the Spirit calmed, Quentin reviewed the ministry activity during quarantine and the virus. He declared that the divine destiny of Greater Faith was in high gear and could not be stopped. He shared his vision, which included new technology investments and new ministries and programs for the church and the community. He wanted to focus less on getting people into the church and more on getting the church out to the people.

"We need to be where the people are hurting. That's not happening out here in the suburbs. We will be doubling our ministry focus in our downtown location," he said.

After the sermon, Quentin held a call for Christian discipleship, and twelve people came forward to be saved. He was shocked to see a familiar silhouette move slowly down the aisle. As she got closer to the front of the church, Quentin recognized his ex-girlfriend Jacqueline Bassett holding the hand of a child who had to be eleven or twelve years old. Quentin had not seen Jacqueline in years. She did not take her eyes off him as she walked down the aisle. Tears flowed down her face as she kneeled at the altar.

Seeing her pulled Quentin out of the Spirit momentarily. He

tried to shake it off, but a quick glance at Vanessa let him know she recognized his ex. He closed his eyes and asked the Lord to help him refocus. He also asked if anyone wanted to join the church. More than twenty people came forward. Quentin was overwhelmed. Twelve new converts and twenty new members caused a shout in the church.

After the prayer, and recitation of Romans 10:9 for those giving their lives to Christ, Quentin was surprised to see Adembe come forward before the offering was taken. He was holding both his children, and though he was masked, Quentin knew he was smiling brightly.

"Is not our God good?" Adembe asked. His staccato baritone voice was loud and full of power. "Our family went through so much during this COVID-19 pandemic. I thought I was going to lose my children *and* my wife. But God had the final say."

The congregation applauded loudly.

"And I want to thank our pastor. He was there with me. The things we did …" He turned, looked at the pastor, and winked. "Our pastor is a praying man, a powerful man of God with the gift of healing flowing through his veins. He made this possible and"—he was just short of tears—"Shalela and I are eternally grateful. But that is not why I am here." He called Shalala up and gave her the babies.

"I am here because we are going to have a special offering. In my country, Ghana, the offering is a celebration. I know we say that here, but we live it in Ghana. We know that we do not have a lot. Maybe we can only bring several ears of corn or some grain, but we are thankful for what God has allowed us to have, no matter how big or small. And we are still able to help those in need. Oh, but we celebrate God in our lives. We dance for Jesus, who is so faithful. We are glad, very, very happy that God has blessed us with the abundance to give. And now we can give on the church's website, Cash App, Zelle, PayPal; there are so many ways that we can give thanks. This is how we do it. Band, give me a groove."

The congas started the beat, followed rhythmically by the bass guitar. The congregation began to clap, sway, and bob their heads as the native beat became a divine dance partner. When Brother Tony hit the organ, the praise elevated. The dance team, now dressed in colorful African print fabric, paraded down each of the three aisles spinning, swaying, and showcasing their gifts of rhythmic movement magic. The African flavor was so thick in the room that Quentin thought he smelled chichinga, a meal he had fallen in love with four years earlier during his trip to Ghana.

As the dancers led the way, each row from the back of the church followed down the aisles to the giving stations at the front of the church. Everyone was in step. Many waved checks, offering envelopes, cash, or their hands. It was a high-praise, joy-filled dance celebration like no offering ever at Greater Faith. The rhythmic pulsation of the ancestors beat the sanctuary like an Akan drum.

Quentin was shocked to see Rev. Jeremiah Jenkins walk slowly by the altar during the offering. Jenkins didn't appear so happy, and he certainly was not basking in the celebration. Jenkins fired an intimidating gaze at Quentin and nodded with a menacing flavor. He put two fingers to his eyes and then pointed those fingers at Quentin, indicating that he was being watched. Quentin knew Jenkins blamed him for losing his episcopal appointment, but nothing could be done about that now. After the offering musical medley and the prayer thanking God for the overflowing offering, Quentin—humbled by the day's blessings—stood to deliver the benediction.

"Y'all really got me this time," he said with a big smile as members of the congregation laughed and applauded. "I want you to give a hand to this awesome worship design team, which created this outstanding, Spirit-filled service, and kept me in the dark during most of the planning. Y'all did real good. I also want to recognize my mother, Essie Dillard. Doesn't she look good this morning?"

She got a standing ovation. She stood and waved, basking in the attention.

"I also want to recognize my dear wife, Vanessa, who was my

rock for the past year as we embarked on this COVID-19 journey. I am so grateful not only for this amazing service but also for how we handled being unable to have a live service and the other challenges that came our way. I can truly say that we are stronger now than we have ever been. Please don't get me wrong. There have been dark times in the past fourteen months. And I don't know if the dark times are over. Thank you for your prayers, but please do not stop praying for Greater Faith and your pastor. We will be organizing new member classes for those who joined this morning, and we are looking forward to greater things with our Lord. Let's pray as we prepare to leave God's house but never God's presence."

The service was a rousing success. People hung around in the sanctuary and church foyer, sticking to each other like bees in a hive. After meeting with visitors and all those who had joined the church, Quentin made his way to his office, greeting and bumping fists with people he had not seen in more than a year along the way. Some he recognized despite their mask; others he was clueless to their identities. But it was great to see the happiness in their eyes. Once in his office, he reclined in his chair. He was exhausted. Members of the ministerial staff came in, laid hands on him, and prayed that his strength would be renewed. After a few minutes of rest, he received a visit from Sister Carretha.

"Sister Cee, you tore it up this morning," he said with a smile. "God has truly restored your voice since your COVID episode."

"I count it all joy, Pastor," she said, moving quickly to a spiritual zone. "I really do. Once I claimed my healing, I was able to bless so many people in that hospital. I spoke to them as God spoke to me. I prayed for so many and laid hands on patients all over the floor I was on. I was there on special assignment; COVID was just my entrance pass. I had to walk through my darkest valley with God so I would be positioned to bring some light into that very dark place. In fact, a couple of people I prayed for joined the church this morning. But I am not here about that. I am here about you. Have you gone to get your help yet?"

Quentin dropped his head. "Sister Cee, I'm really tired."

"Pastor Q, you know God has a plan for you. You laid out a small part of your vision in your sermon today, which was a blessing. But none of that will come to pass if you don't get help. I know it might be embarrassing. I know you don't want the word on the street. But you've got to get help soon. Don't ruin the plan. Don't curtail the expansion. I'll be praying for your swift action."

As she exited the room, leaving an ominous aura in her wake, she placed a business card on Quentin's desk. Just as she closed the door, his office phone rang. Quentin rarely answered the phone after service, but he was moved by the Holy Spirit.

"Good afternoon. I hate to disturb you after you delivered such a powerful word this morning. My name is Davis Devine. I represent By The Wayside Church."

"That's Reverend Roger Clements's church, isn't it?" Quentin asked.

"Well, it was," Devine said, emphasizing each word. "Pastor Clements didn't have a good experience during the virus. He couldn't handle the number of people getting sick, and we lost six people to COVID. That tore him up. And he wasn't well himself. He was battling sickness the entire time. About two months ago, he resigned from his position at the church."

"I did not know that," Quentin said. "I am so sorry. I pray all is well with his soul."

"That's why I'm calling," Devine said. "I've been given the authority by the church leadership council to reach out and give you a… proposition."

Quentin was surprised. "What proposition do you have for me?"

"Well, it started when several of our members came to Greater Faith to participate in the food distribution. They loved it and invited more and more people to be a part of it. Then a few people tuned into your Sunday morning services. We were inspired, and we loved the preaching and teaching. Over the last month, we made a crucial decision for the life of the church. We're independent now, but we want to position ourselves to prosper in the future. And more than half the people who joined Greater Faith this morning were from Wayside. They sorta jumped the gun."

"Jumped the gun?"

"I have been authorized to request that you become the pastor of Wayside Church. We are willing to sign over everything to you, including our building, property, and add a substantial amount to your current salary. And we also have a sizeable endowment."

Quentin's mind developed a brain freeze.

"Are you there, Pastor Dillard?" Devine asked.

"Brother Devine, I can't leave Greater Faith."

"Oh, no. We're not asking you to leave. We're proposing a… merger."

Visions leaped through the freeze in Quentin's mind, almost too many to count at once. "This is certainly a surprise, and I have never heard of an arrangement like this."

"Think about how this sounds: Bishop Quentin E. Dillard…"

That was a Mike Tyson left hook to the face. Quentin had never considered being a bishop. After his recent encounter, he knew that the board of bishops was not a place for him. *Then again*, he thought, *if I am a part of the leadership, I could institute more changes.*

"We're not in a rush," Devine said, "but I would like to send you a proposed agreement in writing. We are willing to meet with you and your church leadership to see if we can agree to an arrangement. But we'd like to hear from you within a week or two."

"Brother Devine, I can't make any promises on when I'll get back to you. I will review your proposal, talk with my family and my team of advisors, and let you know."

"We will anxiously await your call."

Quentin's brain scaled to unknown heights as visions of pastoring two or three additional churches flashed like a psychedelic slideshow. Scenarios, combinations, large audiences, and more ministries flowed through his mind like a mighty river. Someone knocked on his door.

"Come on in."

Jacqueline walked through the door with eyes that melted Quentin and brought back memories that had been suppressed for almost a decade.

"This is J'Quen," she said, staring into Quentin's eyes.

Quentin looked at the young girl whose face seemed strangely familiar. His heart appeared to stop as he looked at Jacqueline and wondered...

Printed in the United States
by Baker & Taylor Publisher Services